A boot tucked ... him over on his back. He looked into the face of Luke Masters. Looked past the rancher's son to the three men he had dimly recognised the night before.

Fargo: the tall, thin man with the hooked nose.

Jude: with the pinto vest and the red hair.

Cotton: the kid with two guns.

'Lift him up,' said Masters.

They lifted him. Jude and Cotton held his arms; Fargo slung an arm around his throat, holding his head back.

And then Luke Masters came in with both his big fists swinging.

They drummed a tattoo of pain over Breed's body, starting low down and working slowly up until they reached his face. He felt his lips split against his teeth, his nose burst blood that ran down over his mouth and shirt in thick streams. One eye closed. Then there was the faint sensation of falling; a reality when his body hit the ground and fresh pain sparked upwards from his side and back. Then more as boots began to pound against him.

Someone laughed. Then someone tilted Breed's chin back and spat on his face.

Luke Masters said, 'You hear me? You got off lucky. You ever come back, I'll kill you. Like I'll kill all yore kind. You tell 'em that.'

BREED:
Slaughter Time

JAMES A. MUIR

SPHERE BOOKS LIMITED
30–32 Gray's Inn Road, London WC1X 8JL

First published by Sphere Books Ltd 1981
Copyright © James A. Muir 1981

Set in Intertype Baskerville

Printed and bound in Great Britain by
©ollins, Glasgow

For two friends on the other side of the fence:
Reg and Nina.

ONE

The man rode hunched over in his saddle, letting the pony choose its own pace. The reins were gripped loosely in his left hand, the right clutching at the horn to hold him in place. A welter of bruises decorated his face, placed so closely together that his features were camouflaged by the interlinking of blackening purple marks. One eye was swollen shut, the other red and puffy above an ugly cut that was thick with congealed blood. More fluid dribblings came from his flattened nostrils and from the cuts where his lips had been mashed back against his teeth. Sweat darkened the armpits and back and chest of his faded linen shirt, and his shoulder-length mane of blond hair hung limp about his collar. Each slow step of the big grey animal he rode brought his teeth together in clenching admission of the pain that wracked his body, producing a fine beading of perspiration across his broad forehead.

He followed the trail slanting up through the trees until it debouched into a canyon that was carpeted with sparse grass, the walls high and white in the afternoon sun, the reflected glare causing him to wince as his good eye watered and dropped salty tears into the cut on his cheek. He followed the canyon down to where a narrow cut bled through to a wider spread of land, then turned north and west. The trail got rocky here, the grass giving way to bare stone that rang loudly under the shod hooves of the grey horse. After a while the trail curved round to follow the path of the descending sun, heading due west through a landscape of jumbled rock that glistened in a myriad eye-watering colours that shimmered and shifted in the radiant light. When he reached a place where a great, sheer wall of white stone lifted up like a curtain dropped from the sky, he turned into a gulley that might once have held a river inside its bare confines, but was now just hard, dry sand. Mesquite and cholla dotted the arid ground, the grey and green of the living plants contrasting dully with the iridescent colouring of the rock. He followed the gulley on to where it turned north, then swung west again into a ravine of dark blue stone.

At the end of the ravine there was a low wall of washed-out shale, pale red against the blue. He climbed it slowly and came over the rim into a shallow canyon that was almost hidden behind a stand of wind oak. The walls of the canyon were no more than fifty feet high. Caves dotted the upper level like the eye sockets of sun-bleached skulls, but along the lower levels there were the remnants of buildings: adobe frontages that jutted out from the cliffs, like boxes stacked one atop the other. Thirty feet up from the ground, the empty adobes were linked by ancient ladders, their wood still good, despite their age. At the bottom, stone steps led to the first terraces, the entrances still guarded by weathered fences and piles of wind-washed boulders.

Mesquite and juniper filled up the interior of the canyon, intercut with wind oak. There was a stream running down the centre, emerging from a small, dark hole in the western face of the rock and disappearing inside a second small, dark hole that was slightly to the south of the eastern side.

The man halted his pony beside the stream and eased his body down from the saddle. The movement caused him fresh pain, and he groaned as he set his moccasined feet on the warm earth and staggered towards the water.

He went down on his knees, more from weakness than voluntary action, and pitched the flat-crowned Sonoran stetson from his head. Then he sunk his face in the water, holding it there as the cool, fast-flowing current washed over the bruises; washed the blood away. He eased

2

his face slowly clear of the stream, panting like a dog, down on all fours like a dog.

But hating like a man.

Hating like warrior of the Chiricahua.

He stood up. Slowly. Painfully. And went over to the grey stallion, hauling the animal away from the stream before it could bloat its belly on excess water. He tethered the horse and slipped the saddle loose, dropping it along with the blanket close to the rock wall. Then he fixed a hobble about the forelegs and eased the harness clear of the proud grey head. After that he stripped off his own garments – the shirt, a pair of close-fitting buckskin pants, and the high moccasins favoured by the Apache peoples – and climbed into the stream.

He lay in the cool water for a long time, feeling the liquid ease the pain with its numbing cold before he climbed out and lay naked in the sun.

His name was Azul.

Or Matthew Gunn.

Or Breed.

It depended on who knew him, and from where they came; even on how they thought of him.

He was the product of a marriage between the Santa Fe trader, Kieron Gunn, and a woman of the Chiricahua Apache, Rainbow Hair. He had been raised as an Apache, yet taught the ways of the whitemen – *the pinda-lick-oyi* – by his father. In the great cathedral in Santa Fe, he had been christened Matthew Gunn, after his father; in the *rancheria* of his mother's people, he was called Azul, for his blue eyes. He was a man born of two races. A man torn between the disparate needs of red and white, belonging fully to neither, understanding both. And often hated for the mixture of blood coursing his veins.

Down along the Border men had given him a new name : Breed.

Some said it spelled death.

Slowly, wary of the bruises that covered, as well as his face, his ribs and belly and back, he climbed to his

3

feet. He pulled on his clothes. Then fastened a gunbelt about his waist. It held a Colt's Frontier model in .45 calibre and a leather sheath containing a wide-bladed Bowie knife. Into the side of his right moccasin he slid the needle-sharp, slender blade of a throwing knife. Then he slid a Winchester rifle in .44-40 calibre from the sheath belted to his saddle and moved off down the canyon; slowly.

He had seen jackrabbits down amongst the foliage at the western end.

He sat against the rock, tearing meat from the roasted carcass of the rabbit. The juices ran hot and stinging against his lips, and the movement of his jaws sent flashes of pain up through his cheeks, into his nose and eyes.

But the food tasted good : it was giving him strength, filling his belly with honest meat and rich, red blood. He looked at the fire, then up at the moon that was shifting imperceptibly across the sky, like a pale and wailing face mourning his hurt.

Soon, he thought. *When this eye opens again and I can move faster. Ten days, maybe. Then I go back.*

He tore the last of the meat from the rabbit and sucked the thin marrow from the bones. He tossed the remnants into the fire and walked slowly over to the stream. Rinsed out his mouth and washed his face. Then went back and banked the fire up before curling into his blanket and sinking into sleep.

Soon, was his last thought : definite; implacable. Relentless as the encroaching approach of death.

His battered lips curved in an ugly smile as he repeated the single word :

Soon.

4

TWO

Mattock was pretty big for a West Texas town.

Backed up against the eastern edge of the Guadalupes, right on the New Mexico line, it got sheltered from the weather by the overhang of the mountains and also got the water from the hills. It was located close enough to the Goodnight-Loving cattle trail that it picked up a fair number of drovers heading northwards out of the high-price cattle country to the south, and found plenty of business from its own ranchers. There was a big corral on the east side, with smaller stock pens around, all fed by a windmill that pumped water up out of the dusty ground into a series of cache tanks. There was a Cattleman's Association office right by the pens, and another – larger – one, inside the town. There was a bank and a stage depot; a saddlery, a stable, a gunsmith's; a dry-goods store and a hardware store; a general store and a saloon; one hotel; one eating house; a marshal's office with a three-cell jail built of brick out back, and a whorehouse.

Mattock was pretty big.

And Jonas Masters was the biggest man in town.

The biggest man in the territory.

Not just in size, though his shoulders were close on twice as wide as most men's, and if he had been able to stand upright he would have topped close to seven feet. His hair was white, very thick, falling down into a beard and moustache that gave his weathered face a patriarchal look, like some prophet out of the Old Testament. His chest and arms and hips were equally wide, in proportion to his height. Only his legs failed to fit the giant image : they were thin, withered inside the black pants he wore, hidden beneath the blanket that covered his wheelchair.

Jonas Masters had commanded a squadron of Texas Volunteers during the War Between The States. He had fought hard and long – and bloodily – from the very outset. Then, at Chandler's Ford, a Minié bullet had hit him in the back, lodging against his spine. For a month he had fought to live, and when the doctors pulled him through, it had been without the use of his legs.

There was no feeling there. Nothing but the dead weight of the two limbs that dangled like rotting stumps from the base of his body. Over the years since the War, they had withered even more, so that now he was not even able to walk on crutches, but confined to the chair he had ordered from St. Louis. Yet, in a curious way, the awful wounding had been a spur that drove Jonas Masters on. He had come out of the War a cripple, too ashamed to return home, selling up instead and putting all his money into cattle. He had foreseen the beef shortage that was destined to hit the newly united States, and invested in land and cows. He had hired good men to guard his land and built a small empire. Along the way a mixed band of Comanche and Kiowa had killed his wife, so now Jonas Masters relied on his son to handle the ranch.

Luke was twenty-five years old, with his father's build and his mother's looks. He was tall and wide and handsome. Perhaps too handsome, for he had sparked up at least three local girls and come running to his father for money without marrying any of them. He preferred to spend his time in the saloon or the cat house : too much time for Jonas' liking; with not enough spent on the ranch. But Jonas went on funding the boy – he still thought of his grown son as a *boy* – and settled his debts and his problems with the same autocratic command that had made him the richest man in the territory. A man who ruled from the throne of his wheelchair, commanding the storekeepers and whores of Mattock like some feudal lord.

Until now.

Until that goddam halfbreed showed up.

Jonas Masters watched the five stud bulls he had shipped in, milling around their individual pens and felt a sudden chill grip his legs. He knew he was imagining it : he couldn't feel anything below his hips. But, by God ! they felt cold still.

Breed rode into Mattock with a chilly north wind trailing his back.

There was no reason for going there other than the fact that he wanted to spend time away from the Mogallons and let the trouble up there die down*. Mattock was as good a place as any to pick, and far enough distant so that he should be safe.

Just like any other travelling man, he booked into the Mattock Palace Hotel. The sign out front said it was the biggest and best from El Paso to Odessa, and his room was comfortable enough. It had a wide bed and a wardrobe; a washstand with a jug of fresh water in the enamel bowl; and what looked like a carpet on the floor. The window opened onto Mainstreet, and the only problem had been the desk clerk who studied his face as he signed the register.

He had signed as Matthew Gunn, and when he spoke English to the clerk, the man had sighed and said, 'Fine. That's all right.'

'Why?' Breed had asked. 'What difference does it make?'

'A lot,' the clerk had answered, blotting the register. 'Injuns ain't exactly welcome here. Nor them related to injuns. On account of Mister Masters' troubles.'

'I never heard of him,' Breed had said. 'What troubles?'

'His wife got took by the Comanch'. They took her an' took her.' The clerk had shrugged, embarrassed. 'Know what I mean? She died. Since then, Mister Masters an' his boy ain't been overly fond of injuns. So — seein' as how he more or less runs this town — I hafta to be careful.'

*See BREED 14: SPANISH GOLD.

The same day Breed had found out how careful.

He had taken a bath and eaten a meal. Checked his horse into the stable, and then gone to the hardware store to buy fresh shells.

The store had a big sign outside, a solid section of wood that was suspended from four metal chains over the sidewalk. It carried a legend scored into the wood with hot irons and black paint. It read: *Caleb Black's Hardware Emporium.* Underneath those words there was a faint etching in white that said: *No Indians or Niggers.*

The store had been empty when he walked in. Forks and hoes and rakes and shovels were stacked against one wall. Heavier equipment was canted either side of a trestle occupying the centre of the room. To the left there was a glass-fronted counter with guns set out on green cloth. As he went in, a bell had rung from its stanchion over the door and a girl with long blonde hair and dark grey eyes had come out from the back. She was wearing a pale blue dress that looked a little too small, as though she had worn it a long time, enough for her figure to fill faster than the dress could accommodate.

She had smiled at him.

'Can I help you?'

He had bought six boxes of cartridges, the .45 to .44-40 that fitted both the Colt and the Winchester, and was handing over his money when the man walked in.

He was tall, close on three inches higher than Breed. Wearing a dark blue shirt that looked like it had been washed and ironed that same day. Stovepipe chaps covered his legs, buttoned up with fancy silver conchos that matched the chasings on his gunbelt. He carried a Colt's Peacemaker in the holster and a broad-rimmed, silver-banded stetson in his left hand.

When he saw the girl smiling at Breed, his face froze. It might have been a handsome face, once; a few years back. Now it was fleshed out, getting jowly around the chin and soft on the cheeks. The eyes were black and angry, carrying more life than the small roll of fat that sat over the gunbelt.

'Sarah!' It sounded like a command. 'What the hell you think you're doing?'

'Serving a customer, Luke,' the girl had said. 'What else?'

Her smile switched off as she said it, then came back on as she looked at Breed.

It was the first time he met Luke Masters.

'I don't like it.' The big man stood a few feet clear of Breed. 'He's got an injun look to him.'

'You don't own all of Mattock,' the girl had said. 'I can serve anyone I like.'

'Like?' Masters had grunted. 'How can anyone like a goddam halfbreed injun?'

He fastened his right fist over the butt of his Colt as he said it, then looked again at Breed.

'Word of warning, injun. Pay for what you want, then get out. Today.'

Breed had looked back into the angry eyes and said, 'When I'm ready. Not before.'

The man's face had curved in a tight, unpleasant smile. 'I'm Luke Masters, feller.'

Breed had said nothing, just scooped the boxes of shells into the gunny sack the girl handed him.

'You hear me, feller?' There was a tight edge of anger in Masters' voice. Like he wasn't used to being ignored. 'I said I'm Luke Masters.'

'Nice name,' Breed had grunted. 'That why you keep repeating it?'

Masters' face had gone pale under the tan, his eyes narrowing as his chin jutted forwards in an expression oddly close to a pout.

'Luke,' the girl had said warningly, 'don't make trouble. Please?'

'Ain't me, Sarah.' Masters came up to the counter, positioning himself on Breed's left. 'It's him. Hell! He reeks of injun. Got the sign on him like the red stripes on

9

a barber pole.'

Breed had turned then, the gunny sack swinging loosely in his left hand, his right close to the Colt on his waist.

'So?' His voice was flat; impassive. Only his eyes betrayed the mounting irritation: they were cold and clear, like a winter sky.

'So we got rules here in Mattock,' grated Luke. 'No injuns. That includes 'breeds.'

'Luke!' Sarah had intervened again. 'He just wants to buy shells. He's got money. Leave him be.'

'Where'd he get it?' Luke had sneered. 'Off some murdered whiteman? Never did know of a 'breed could earn a honest dollar.'

'I earned it,' Breed had said slowly, the explanation prompted by the pleading look in the girl's grey eyes. 'Honestly.'

'Yeah?' Luke's lip had curled in an expression of contemptuous disbelief, but when he saw Breed's face his hand had come clear of the pistol. 'Maybe. Makes no difference – we still got rules.'

'Who makes them?' Breed had challenged. 'You?'

'Goddam right!' Luke had squared his shoulders then, as though trying to find authority in his size. 'You ever hear o' the Box M?' Without waiting for an answer, he had continued, 'Me and my Pa own it. Like we own most o' this town. So, yeah: we do make the rules.'

'I got a rule of my own,' Breed had said; slowly, his accent guttural as the anger mounted. 'I don't let people push me around.'

The paleness had left Masters' face then, replaced by a suffusion of red. His dark eyes had got very big, bulging in anger and disbelief. Breed had ignored him, touching his hat brim to the girl as he turned and walked casually to the door. It swung open with a faint creak of the hinges that was very loud in the sudden silence. He was part-way through before Luke Masters found his voice again, and when it came, it was harsh with rage.

'You best heed what I told you, 'breed. Get the hell outta Mattock.'

Breed had paused, not bothering to look back: 'Or?'

'Or you suffer the consequences.'

The door had swung shut on the last syllable, leaving the big man glaring apoplectically at the dusty glass.

Breed had gone over to the eating house. It was about three-quarters full with cowboys and storekeepers. No one tried to stop him eating, but most of the diners gave him a long, hard look and there was a sudden lull in the buzz of conversation. He chose a table at the far end of the room, set in the angle of the wall between the serving hatch and a window. A fat Mexican woman with her greasy hair fastened in two thick plaits shoved a mug in front of him and filled it with coffee. Her luminous black eyes caught his, and she made a little clucking sound, shaking her head slightly the way a woman might, watching a headstrong child doing something it shouldn't.

He ordered steak, with greens and hash browns. When the steak came it overlapped the sides of the plate and he cut into it wondering if it had come from a Box M steer. The conversations had started up again, but every so often someone would turn to glance surreptitiously at the solitary figure down the far end of the room. There was an air of expectancy in the place, of almost palpable tension, like the nerve-tingling anticipation that precedes a big electric storm. Breed was aware of it, and ignored it. Luke Masters had spelled out the conditions governing Mattock, and it was pretty obvious that they mostly held. The easy thing to do – the sensible thing – would have been to pay for his meal and fetch his gear from the hotel, put it on his horse and ride away. To some town that wasn't so fervently hostile to Indians and half-breeds.

But he had been in too many similar situations. Too often insulted for the Apache blood coursing his veins. Blood of which he was proud. He was a man, a human being, he had money: he had the right to go where he wanted.

He remembered something his father had told him, when he was around thirteen years old . . .

You'll hit problems, Matt, his father had said one day when they were building a corral to trap a small herd of broncos that contained two fine mares and a superb stallion, *being part white. Or part red. Whichever. There'll be folks take offence. They'll figger they're better than you. Figger having pure blood makes them right, an' you having mixed blood, wrong.*

Does it? the boy had asked, remembering how sometimes an Apache youth – usually one he had beaten in a game, or in one of the tests that were bringing them to full manhood – would taunt him with the fact that he was not pure Chiricahua.

No, his father had replied. *Of course it don't. What makes a man right or wrong, what makes him a man, is what's in his soul. Not what's in his veins, or the colour of his skin. There's good Apaches, an' there's bad Apaches. There's folk who say the blacks ain't as good as whites, but I've known black men I'd trust a whole lot farther than some whites. It's what's inside a man. You need remember that – you're as good as any man, an' if anyone tries to tell you different, you stand up to them. You show them.*

He had remembered. He remembered it now, and decided that he would quit Mattock in his own time.

He ate the last of the steak and nodded his thanks as the Mexican woman set a hunk of bilberry pie before him. She poured cream, leaning across the table so that her bulk hid the rest of the room, her pendulous breasts sagging inside the grubby blouse.

'*Cuidarse, hombre.*' Her voice was soft, wary. 'Be careful.'

'*Por qué?*' Breed replied in the same language. 'Why?'

The woman's lashes fluttered, her eyes flicking to either side as if she was afraid of being overheard. 'This town does not like your kind. The last one, they rode him out on a pole. After . . .'

She broke off as a hoarse voice bellowed from the kitchen : '*Maria! Donde estás?*'

Maria stood up quickly and hurried to collect the waiting order. Breed finished his meal and dropped coins on the table, then he stood up and walked slowly out of the eating house. The more he heard about Mattock, the less he liked. And the more determined he became to stay until he – and he alone – was ready to leave.

He decided to get a drink and began to walk down Mainstreet in the direction of the saloon. As he passed the hotel, someone called to him.

'Mister Gunn?'

He turned, looking into the shadowed entrance of the two-storey building. The clerk was standing just inside the door. He was wearing striped pants and a matching vest over a stiff-collared white shirt with a wide, blue tie. The vest and shirt were open, rents down the front of the cotton showing where buttons had ripped loose. The fancy tie was askew, the knot dragged loose. The clerk was holding onto the door-frame like a man in need of support, with his left hand pressed hard against his belly. A bruise was spreading over one eye and there was a smear of blood at the corner of his mouth.

'Mister Gunn?' he repeated nervously. 'I hafta ask you to leave.'

Breed looked past the man to where his gear was dumped carelessly in the centre of the lobby.

'There'll be no bill.' The clerk said it fast, like a man looking for an excuse to avoid trouble. 'Just take your stuff and go. Please?'

Breed didn't move. Instead he fixed his cold stare back on the clerk's face and asked, 'Why?'

'Oh, Jesus!' The clerk worried at his lip, then winced as his teeth caught a split. 'Luke Masters says so.'

'And Luke Masters makes the rules here.' Breed's voice was cold now as his eyes. 'He own this hotel?'

'His pa owns a share,' said the clerk. 'He owns a piece of just about everything in town. It's more'n my job's worth to argue.'

'He don't own me,' grated Breed. 'Where do I find him?'

'Jonas?' The clerk sounded amazed. 'Or Luke?'

'Seems like it's Luke doing the ordering,' Breed said. 'Him.'

The clerk swallowed hard, his eyes getting wide as was possible with the bruise swelling one almost closed. 'The Lucky Lady, I guess.'

'Thanks.' Breed turned away, walking towards the saloon.

It was a long, low building, part wood and part adobe. Dirty windows flanked the batwing doors, the glass etched with curlicued letters that advertised beer and whisky. Inside, it was warm and dim, the air thick with the mingled odours of liquor and tobacco smoke and sweat. The plank floor was covered with sawdust and a long bar ran the full length of one wall. Shelves filled with bottles and glasses backed the bar, their length broken only by the open space at the centre where a crude painting of a large-breasted woman wearing a white nightgown that wasn't quite off her bosom held pride of place. There were two bartenders serving drinks to around a dozen men who looked like cowhands, and three card games going on at the tables that broke up the span of the floor. Across from the painting there was an upright piano, its wood scarred and ringed with the marks of glasses. A man in a striped shirt and a black derby was pounding the keys more or less in time with his voice. He was singing something about a gal called Sal, who gave her all.

He faltered slightly as the batwings swung shut behind Breed, then picked up the tempo again, slightly louder.

> Yes, Sal was a gal who gave her all,
> To a no-account man called Hank.
> And Hank was a man who liked 'em tall
> And ready to give him a . . .

The next few words got lost behind the sudden throb of conversation, and Breed shut them off as he went up to the bar.

'Whisky.'

The barkeep looked at him, licking his lips. He was short and fat, with pudgy cheeks and a thick moustache. His watery eyes swung away from Breed's face to scan the room, coming to rest on a point midway down from the piano. Breed followed his gaze and saw Luke Masters staring at him with his mouth gaping open in surprise. The big man was seated at a table with three others. They looked a little like working cowhands, but more like gunmen. One was tall and thin, with black hair and mean little eyes that were too small for the hooked nose jutting beak-like from his angular face. He wore blue denims and a black shirt. A Colt was hung butt-forwards on his right hip. Seated left of him was a square-built, stocky man wearing a pinto vest over a red shirt that was a shade darker than his flaming hair. He might have been fat, but from where Breed stood it looked more like muscle. He carried a Colt in a plain holster tied down on the right leg of his brown pants. The third man looked younger, closer to Luke Masters' age. His mouse-coloured hair and open face added to the impression of youth, and his faded blue shirt and equally faded blue denims made him look more like a cowboy than the others. The impression was jarred by the twin ivory-handled Remingtons hung low on his hips.

'Whisky,' Breed repeated.

'I ain't sure.' The barkeep's eyes shifted between the halfbreed and Luke Masters. 'We got rules.'

'I heard.' Breed dropped a coin on the bar. 'Hearing so much about them makes me thirsty.'

'Uh . . .' The barkeep fidgeted with a cloth and a glass that was already clean. 'I . . . uh . . .'

'Don't make me ask again.' Breed's voice was low and very cold. It did something to the barkeep's nerves so that the glass suddenly fragmented under his furious scrubbing. He yelped, dropping the pieces as he stuck a thumb in his mouth and began to suck on the blood. Abruptly, like a man coming to a decision he didn't like

15

taking, he slid a fresh glass across the bar and followed it with a bottle.

Breed tilted the bottle over the glass, then lifted the whisky to his lips. The saloon got quiet then, the background noise falling away like water draining from a holed bucket. For a few seconds the piano went on tinkling, the pianist's voice echoing loud against the stillness.

> *So Sal told Hank,*
> *You ain't no good,*
> *You made me do what a girl never should . . .*

The song tailed off. A key, struck in discord, jangled and throbbed into silence. A chair scraped against the floor and boot heels thudded on the planks. Breed drained the glass, looking fixedly at the garish painting, listening to the footsteps coming closer.

'You been told,' said a familiar voice. 'Now you had a drink, too. That's more'n most of yore kind get. Now go collect your saddle an' ride out.'

Breed set the glass down gently. The two bartenders were both at the far end now, looking like brothers twinned by the nervous anticipation on their faces. One had his hands under the counter. Where a shotgun might be hidden.

Breed turned to face Luke Masters.

'I got a thirst,' he said. 'And like I told you : I'll leave when I'm ready.'

Masters' handsome face flushed, and for a moment Breed thought it might all end there. He felt confident of killing the big man, but he wasn't sure he could get out of the saloon. Not alive. Masters first, he thought, he's big enough to block the others. Then whoever draws next. One of the three at the table. Maybe all three. Then run for the hotel – get the rifle. Then he saw the faint hint of fear lurking behind Luke's dark eyes. It was difficult to pinpoint exactly : something to do with the way the pupils were dilated, their focus shifting slightly from side to side. But it was there, and he knew that Luke Masters was relying on his reputation and his size to bluff his way through : he knew that Luke Masters, for all his bravado, was afraid.

Masters licked his lips.

'I said now!'

Breed lifted the bottle. Filled the glass again. He smiled into the cattleman's flushed face. It wasn't a pleasant smile.

'Try to stop me,' he murmured, too low for anyone but Luke to hear, 'and I'll kill you.'

There was a finality in his tone that left no room for doubt. It penetrated Masters' anger, wiping the flush from his face so that the cheeks got pale, the points of the cheekbones highlighted by twin spots of bright red. Luke swallowed and took a pace backwards. Breed raised the glass and tossed the whisky down.

'Jude! Fargo! Cotton!' Luke's voice was hoarse, the words coming from a dry throat. 'We got trouble.'

The three men climbed to their feet. Now it became obvious they knew a lot more about gunplay than they did about cows. They spread out, the thin man moving to the right, the redhead to the left. The youngster stayed at the centre, moving slightly sideways so that he could look past Masters. The play was classic, obvious in its simplicity : not even a fast gun could get off more than two shots before one of them downed him.

Breed went on smiling into Luke's face and dropped his glass on the bar. It bounced and rotated on its own axis, setting up a thin rattling that whirred to a slow stop as he said, 'I'll still kill you.'

Then the batwings flung open and a voice said, 'No you won't. There'll be no gunplay.'

He eased back against the edge of the bar, twisting his body far enough round that he could see the newcomer and still keep Luke in sight. The man was around his own height, a grey stetson shading most of his face, a thick brown moustache covering a lot of the rest. He wore grey pants and a white shirt. There was a Colt holstered on his waist and a Winchester carbine in his hands. The hammer was back and the muzzle was pointed midway between Breed and Masters. A five-pointed gold star was pinned to the breast pocket of his shirt. It reflected little dancing points of light into the room.

'He's a halfbreed, Con,' said Masters. 'I told him what the rules are.'

'He pay for his likker?' asked the peace officer.

The barkeep who had served Breed nodded.

'Then he ain't broke no law,' said the sheriff. 'Leave him be.'

'Taggart!' Luke's voice regained its authority as the immediate threat of death retreated. 'You're pushin' it.'

'Shut yore mouth, Luke.' Taggart sounded almost casual. 'You make too much trouble. Some day you're gonna take it too far, an' then not even yore daddy's money's gonna bail you out.'

Breed's smile eased down into a grin of contempt. He set his glass upright and reached for the bottle again.

'What the hell you think you're doin'?' Taggart's voice got cold. 'Set that bottle down an' keep yore hands where I can see them.'

Conscious of the Winchester pointed at his midriff, Breed set the bottle down and turned to face the sheriff. Taggart didn't look afraid or angry; just calm and slightly bored.

'You the one Sarah told me about? Had a run in with Luke over to the hardware store?'

Breed nodded.

'All right, mister.' Taggart eased sideways, clearing a passage to the door. 'You got yore shells an' you had a drink. Now fetch yore gear outta the hotel an' ride on. I'm postin' you undesirable.'

'Why?' Breed asked.

'Because I'm the law an' you're trouble,' said Taggart. 'You go find some other town to do yore drinkin' in. You ain't welcome here, an' I ain't about to ride herd on no redskin.'

'That's real white of you,' rasped Breed.

'It's a whiteman's town,' answered Taggart. 'That's how it is.'

'Maybe I should paint it red,' murmured Breed.

But under the threat of the carbine he moved towards the door.

THREE

'Might be you owe me thanks.' Taggart kept the Winchester pointed at Breed as the blond-haired man fastened his saddle in place on the grey stallion. 'Could be I just saved yore life.'

'Thanks,' grunted Breed, the word coming out like an insult. 'Thanks a lot.'

For a moment, Taggart's calm wavered. He shrugged : a barely perceptible movement that did nothing to shift the aim of the carbine. One corner of his mouth lifted in a cynical grin.

'Look, feller, I'm the law in Mattock. It's my job to keep the peace, an' the way Luke an' his pa feel about injuns, that means keeping folk like you out.'

'And the Masters own the town,' grunted Breed. 'Including you.'

Taggart ignored the jibe. 'I get elected,' he said, 'by a vote. How folks vote depends pretty much on what Jonas tells 'em. Most of 'em depend on the Box M for their living, so I'm doin' what any legally appointed officer does : representing the people.'

'And keeping your job.' Breed swung into the saddle. 'Without bucking the bosses.'

Something that might have been a guilty frown passed over the lawman's regular features.

'They'd have killed you,' he said. 'I don't know how fast you are, but there ain't no one can beat them three Luke keeps with him. You best count yourself lucky you got out alive. Hell ! they didn't even beat up on you.'

He stared at Breed, brown eyes meeting the cold blue gaze, then shook his head. 'Just get the hell outta here. There's a place called Valverde two days south. Mex town : they'll serve you there.'

'They served me here,' said Breed, softly.

'They'd have killed you here, too,' grunted Taggart. 'Don't come back.'

He kept the Winchester pointed on the halfbreed's back as he paced behind the grey horse, down Mainstreet, to the southern edge of the town.

'Remember what I told you,' he called as he halted in the shade of an adobe building. 'Don't come back.'

Breed drove his heels against the pony's flanks and lifted the animal to a trot without looking back. He rode out through the flat expanse of sun-baked prairie, a hard core of anger churning inside him. It was tempting to circle round and return to Mattock, but a core of commonsense that was harder than the nub of his anger persuaded him against it. Taggart – whatever Breed might think of him – was right : backed by the three gunmen, Luke Masters would see him killed. And the sheriff had seemed hard enough to back his promises with more than just words.

He followed the southwards trail.

Con Taggart waited at the edge of Mattock until the halfbreed got hidden behind the heat haze shimmering off the arid ground. The Valverde trail went through a section of Box M land, but it was mostly waterless semi-desert that only supported cattle in the Spring, so it wasn't very likely the halfbreed would meet any of the Masters hands *And hell!*, Taggart thought, *I done my best. I saved him from a beating, or worse. Didn't I?* He tugged a cheroot from his shirt pocket and stuck it in his mouth. Struck a match on his belt. Sucked in the smoke. And began to walk back into town.

Sarah Black met him halfway down Mainstreet, and his frown faded into a smile.

'He's gone,' he said. 'Lord knows why I gotta look after yore stray dogs, but I stopped Luke an' his crew shootin' him.'

The girl smiled. 'Got coffee just brewed, Con. You want some?'

Taggart looked at her face and her figure and wondered if she meant something more than coffee. 'Sure,' he said. 'Thanks.'

'Bastard!'

Luke Masters swallowed whisky.

'Goddam bastard.'

'Halfbreed,' said Jude. 'They're all the same.'

'Don't see how a whiteman would go with a squaw,' said Cotton. 'Not unless she was in a whorehouse.'

'He was lucky,' muttered Luke. 'If Taggart hadn't come in . . .'

'He needs killin',' said Fargo. 'Needs a lesson taught.'

'Injuns rape white women,' said Cotton. 'But the kids turn out dark. Look like injuns. He musta been one off a squaw. They're lighter. Get more white blood from the man's seed.'

'Could use a lesson,' Fargo grumbled. 'Might be best not to kill him. Just hurt him. So he lives to tell the others.'

'Goddam lucky fer him Taggart came in when he did. Saved his goddam life.'

Luke picked up the bottle and saw that it was empty. He shouted for another. The thinner of the two barkeeps came over and lifted the three drained bottles clear before placing the fresh one on the table.

'Wonder where Con sent him,' slurred Jude.

'Valverde, I reckon,' said Cotton. 'Ain't nowhere else closer than a week.'

'They got some fine Mex whores there,' said Fargo. 'I had me a couple a while back.'

'Better'n Annie's?' Cotton's mouth hung slack at the thought. 'Better'n that French girl?'

'French girl, shit!' said Fargo. 'She ain't been closer to France than New Orleans. Creole, her.'

'That's like a nigger, ain't it?' asked Jude. 'You mean

22

we been fuckin' a nigger?'

'Ain't nothin' wrong with fuckin' a nigger,' chuckled Luke. 'It's what comes out after that counts.'

They all laughed. They usually did when Luke Masters cracked a joke.

The fresh bottle got emptied three-quarters down and they fell silent. The saloon had emptied out and the barkeeps were emptying the spittoons and sweeping the floor. The air was thick with smoke.

'I ain't had a Mex girl in some time,' said Fargo. 'Had two the last time. At the same time.'

'Jesus!' said Cotton. 'All three o' you? In bed? All at once?'

Fargo laughed. 'You got a lot o' learnin' to do, boy.'

Cotton said, 'Why don't we go down there? Get us a piece or two?'

'Hey,' said Jude, 'that sounds like a nice idea. How about it, Luke?'

Luke Masters looked up from the dregs of his whisky: 'Valverde? Ain't that where the 'breed's headed?'

'Sure,' said Fargo. 'Might be we'll catch him on the way.'

'All right,' said Luke. 'Let's go.'

They emptied their glasses and stumbled out of the saloon. Over in the stable, a Mexican sweeper told them what he had heard of Marshal Taggart's conversation with Breed. A few minutes later they were driving their horses hard down the Valverde trail.

The land was flat and wide and empty. Night had closed down with the abrupt cessation of day's light that marks the south-western plains, the sun descending like a great burning ball of fire behind the western horizon, lining the sky with striations of red and gold and green as the darker blue of night lifted like a rising curtain from the farther horizon. Stars prickled from the blue, and a huge, yellow-green moon lifted sluggish into the sky. It filled the land with a pale, phosphorescent light that dimmed the flames of Breed's fire, transforming the flickering yellow glow to a ghostly radiance that alternated with the moonlight to throw fantastic shadows back against the cactus and the dark, moon-washed ground.

Breed chewed on the jerky stored in his saddle-bags. There was just enough to take him through to Valverde, and he might find game along the way, if he wanted to take out the time to hunt. For now, he was content to chew on the preserved meat – with the Chiricahua, he had gone longer and hungrier without any food at all.

He washed down the last of the mouthful with water from his canteen, then banked the fire and stretched back against his saddle, tugging the blanket over him as somewhere off to the west a coyote howled at the rising moon.

Sometime around midnight something woke him. It might have been the cessation of the night-time sounds, or the intrusion of a new – unnatural – sound. It was impossible to tell : he just woke, with his right hand fastening on the butt of the Colt. He sat up; listening.

Somewhere close by there was a scuffling movement, followed closely by what might have been a horse snorting through a cupped hand.

He pushed the blanket aside and dropped the Colt into the holster. Lifted the Winchester. The rifle's action made a loud *click* as the lever sprang down and then up.

He rose to his feet.

And a rope landed over his shoulders.

Instinct threw him back against the pull of the lariat, taking off the slack so that he had a chance to wriggle loose as he turned the rifle and triggered a shot into the darkness that had now overtaken the moon. Muzzle flash illuminated a tall figure, pale-faced under a black hat and above a black shirt.

Fargo laughed and drew the rope tight again.

Breed's movement had slipped it clear of his shoulders, but the shifting of his rifle had settled it around his neck. He gasped as the oiled leather slid through the hondo to fasten, noose-like, on his throat.

A second rope caught the barrel of the Winchester and yanked it from his hands as he was levering a second shell into the breech.

He got up on his knees and hurled himself forwards, fighting to gain sufficient purchase so that he could reach the Colt before the tightening hondo crushed his windpipe. At the same time, his left hand dropped to his belt, seeking the hilt of the Bowie knife.

Gun and blade came clear at the same time. One spat flame at the man holding the rope, the other lifted up to slash at the plaited cords.

The Bowie was sharp. It cut the rawhide lariat easy as slicing butter. The rope parted and Fargo staggered back, off-balanced so that the Colt's bullet tore air an inch past his face.

Then something hard and heavy crashed against the halfbreed's legs and something even heavier slammed into his back. He went down on his face, tasting sand in his mouth as a boot landed on his wrist and ground it down into the ashes of the fire. The dying embers singed the hairs on his wrist and he twisted round and back, cocking the Colt as he turned.

A boot slammed against his wrist and the bullet flew wide. Then the same boot came back and landed on his arm, pinning it to the ground as a second smashed down against the hand clutching the knife.

Pain shafted through his arms and he lifted his legs, trying to kick the men pinning him to the ground. Someone laughed and swiped the stock of a rifle across his face. His legs doubled over his belly, then straightened, and the stock came back, ramming down against his midriff like a pile-driver. Black pain flooded his mind as the stock lifted and descended again, this time between his legs, bringing a roaring red column of agony up from his groin, through his stomach, into his mind and mouth and eyes and nose.

There was darkness.

When it went away, he hurt. He opened his eyes slowly; carefully. They looked on sand. There was a small, black ant crawling over the sand. It was moving towards a wide puddle of red that was soaking into the sand. The red was very close to his face: he recognised it as blood. Then realised it was coming from his nose.

He spat, and someone said, 'He's awake.'

'Good.'

A boot tucked against his chest and turned him over on his back. He looked up into the face of Luke Masters. Looked past the rancher's son to the three men he had dimly recognised the night before.

Fargo: the tall, thin man with the hooked nose.

Jude: with the pinto vest and the red hair.

Cotton: the kid with the two guns.

'Lift him up,' said Masters. 'Get the bastard on his feet.'

They lifted him. Jude and Cotton held his arms; Fargo slung an arm around his throat, holding his head back.

And then Luke Masters came in with both his big fists swinging.

They drummed a tattoo of pain over Breed's body, starting low down and working slowly up until they reached his face. He felt his lips split against his teeth, his nose burst blood that ran down over his mouth and shirt in thick streams. One eye closed. After a while the pounding stopped and he heard Masters say, 'All right. Let him go.' Then there was the faint sensation of falling; a reality when his body hit the ground and fresh pain sparked upwards from his side and back. Then more as boots began to pound against him. He rolled into a ball, a foetal shape that curled his legs up to protect his genitals and his hands around his head.

After a while the pounding stopped, and through the red mist that clouded his mind he heard something drop close beside him. Light shone off a glassy surface and there was the faint smell of whisky. A voice that sounded like it belonged to Luke Masters said, 'All right. Leave him.'

Another voice said, 'We goin' to Valverde, Luke?'

'Hell! why not? I could use me a good whore.'

Someone laughed. Then someone tilted Breed's chin back and spat on his face.

Luke Masters said, 'You hear me? You hear me, you goddam injun squaw seed? You got off lucky. You ever come back, I'll kill you. Like I'll kill all yore kind. You tell 'em that.'

There was more laughter. And the sound of men mounting horses. The drumming of the hooves against the ground echoed loud in Breed's ears. He rolled awkwardly sidewards and watched them ride away. A cloud of dust got diffused by the empty whisky bottle resting close to his face. The glass fragmented the sun's light so that the vision of dust and stamping hooves got lost behind a flickering pattern of brilliant light that seemed to pierce down into his mind and coalesce into the raw, aching hole of pain that was consuming his body.

Time passed. He wasn't sure how long or how much. Wasn't even sure that he could tell it right or see it straight. There were periods of light and periods of darkness, but they might be the result of the pain still washing through his body.

All he knew for sure was the fire had gone out and the grey stallion was snickering anxiously. And those things might have been because the horse was worried, or because Masters and his friends had doused the fire.

He eased his hand slowly into the ashes: cold. Not wet or disturbed; just cold.

He rolled over, groaning as the movement flashed fresh lances of pain through his body, and looked up at a bright sky that didn't quite focus until he realised one of his eyes was closed. He touched it. And winced as the touch sent fresh pain into his brain.

He spat dry blood from between his teeth and got up on his hands and knees. The sand under his face spun round and he closed the one eye that he could close until the ground came into focus again. He couldn't tell if the column of ants was really lead by the first one he had seen, but they were working a whole lot busier on the blood, twin columns working busily back and forth from the puddles like well-organised armies raiding an unexpected supply store.

Getting up on his feet was a whole lot harder. He fell over three times before he got to the grey horse, and then needed to use the animal's bulk to lever himself upright as he slung the saddle on its back and fastened the thing in place.

He was surprised to find his guns left with him, and grateful for the drunken abandon, or arrogant carelessness, or whatever that had made Luke Masters forget a prime rule : kill the enemy, don't leave him alive to come after you.

But maybe Luke Masters didn't know that *Apache* meant, in the language of the tribes, *enemy*.

It took him a long time to get up on the grey horse, because the animal was nervous, frightened by the smell of blood – and maybe also the smell of hate – coming off him, but he climbed into the saddle in the end and then turned the animal back towards the distant-bulking shadows of the Guadalupes and began to ride, painfully, slowly, to a place he knew where he could rest up.

Until he came back.

FOUR

Breed hunkered down on the flat terrace fronting an adobe halfway up the cliff. A small fire blackened the sun-washed stone at his feet, the embers surmounted by the carcass of a prairie chicken set on a wooden spit. From time to time he prodded the roasting bird with the point of the Bowie knife, watching the juices spurt out and sputter in the fire. After a while, he lifted the bird away from the flames and began to carve chunks of meat from the breast.

He ate most of the bird, then wrapped what was left in leaves and carried it back into the adobe. The building was cool and very quiet. It had about it the calm distance of time, a stillness like the tranquillity of an old church, as though the ages had permeated the rock to leave an aura of peace. The door was low, framed by pieces of wind-weathered timber that had been set into the original masking of brick and plaster, flanked on one side by a rectangular window. It opened on a single room that ran back into the natural facing of the cliff so that a kind of arch divided the room in two. Beyond the arch, it went back for about twelve feet before another opening presented itself. Beyond this, there was a second room — really a cave, with a platform carved from the rock where a bed might be made, and stone shelves cut into the walls. Most of the adobes were built exactly the same, though some were slightly larger, some smaller. All were empty, scoured over the years of whatever detritus the original inhabitants might have left behind.

Old Sees-The-Fox had shown Breed the place years before, pointing it out as a good hiding place; a refuge.

They had been chasing a bunch of Comanches who had

crossed into Apache territory on a horse-stealing raid. The attackers had driven off close on fifteen head of Chiricahua ponies from a *rancheria* linked to Azul's by ties of blood and marriage. The chief – a warrior called Dancing Pony had asked for help, and Sees-The-Fox had chosen Azul and four other young men to go with him. They had trailed the Comanches for nine days, the hunt culminating in a running fight that left two Chiricahua wounded and six of the horse thieves dead. Returning towards Apacheria, they had rested up inside the canyon.

I do not know who built these houses, old Sees-The-Fox had said. *My father showed them to me when I was a boy, younger than you. They are very old, maybe from the time before even the Spanish came. Not many people dare come here now because they think there are ghosts here. Maybe they are right, but I think that if there are ghosts, they are Apache ghosts, and look friendly on us. Whatever, it is a good place to hide. If you ever need to hide.*

I'll not hide, the young man had said, in his pride. *Not from the Nemmenna or the pinda-lick-oyi. Not from anyone.*

Sees-The-Fox had chuckled and answered : *No one can see his path that far in front. There is nothing cowardly in hiding when you need to. Not if you need time before you go back to repay the debt that made you hide. Going back is the important thing, and waiting is not the same as running.*

Breed understood that better now.

He set the remnants of the prairie chicken on a stone ledge and went back into the sunlight. He clambered down the worn steps of the terrace to the ground below, moving with relative ease : his bruises were fading, and the cracked ribs were knitting back together. He looked down the canyon to where the grey stallion was penned inside a makeshift corral of thorn and mesquite, close to the source of the stream. The big horse looked up as he approached, snickering a greeting and presenting its head for attention. He stroked the velvet muzzle and scratched at the ears. The horse pawed the ground, ducking its head: it was anxious to run, needing exercise.

It was close on two weeks since Luke Masters and his cronies had ambushed the halfbreed, and the journey to the hidden canyon had taken around three days. Breed couldn't be sure exactly how long; for most of the ride he had been barely conscious, doing little more than steer the horse in the right direction. Consequently the animal was getting restless.

He came to a fast decision. Ducking under the fence, he slung the saddle on the grey's back and fixed the bridle in place. Then, holding the reins, he shouldered the barrier away and climbed into the saddle. The horse snorted once, and took off down the canyon at a rising gallop. Breed let it run, giving it its head until they reached the far end and he turned the reins, swinging the pony round to charge back down the length of the rough grass. The fluid motion of the animal simultaneously soothed and hurt him. The pounding hooves sent sparking memories of the beating up through his body, but the sheer joy of being back in the saddle overcame the pain. He rode for almost an hour, criss-crossing the canyon until the sun was fading behind the western rimrock and the bottom was in shadow.

When he dismounted and led the horse back into the corral, he was aching. He turned the animal loose to roll on the grass and went over to the stream, stripping off his clothes. His ribs and belly were still discoloured, the bruises yellowing into a striated pattern of colour that spread across his midriff and sides like a mosaic. Where the boots had stamped on his wrists, there were darker markings like purple-black bracelets. On the surface of the water, his reflection gave back an image of a face rendered ugly by the punches. The gash beneath his eye was healed to a thin red line that cut over the blackish-green of the fading swelling. His lips still looked unnaturally large, laced with a tracery of cuts, and the rest of his skin seemed darker than was normal.

He waded into the water and stretched full length, letting it flow over him, washing away the sweat and the aches. He stayed there until he began to shiver, then climbed out and rolled on the grass the same way the horse had done before standing up with his face turned towards the setting sun. Then he pulled on his clothes and ambled leisurely to where he had set traps.

Two rabbits were snared. He killed them swiftly with sharp chopping motions of his right hand, then took the bodies up to the adobe. He slit the bellies and scooped out the internal organs, saving the hearts and kidneys. Then he skinned the carcasses and put them inside. The hides and entrails he carried up to the highest level, clambering onto the roof of the topmost adobe and hurling the bloody remains up onto the rocks. In the morning the buzzards would come down and clear them away.

It was close on full dark in the canyon by the time he was finished, and he went over to the corral to light a small fire in front of the fence. It was unlikely that prowling coyotes would venture into the canyon now that it was freshly impregnated with man smell, but he was not prepared to risk losing the grey stallion. He banked the fire so that it would burn through the night, then returned to the adobe and built his own small pyre up to full life.

The sun was faded all the way down behind the rimrock as he squatted with the remains of the prairie chicken in his hands and ate the last of the bird with wild onions and greens taken from what might once – a long, long time ago – have been a vegetable garden.

The moon rose, spreading a pale, cold light over the canyon. It shone on the face of the cliff opposite, shading the openings of the windows and doors of the adobes so that they resembled the blank sockets of bleached skulls. It was, he thought, a good place for ghosts. A very old, very lonely place. Not unfriendly : rather, a place for kindred spirits, a place where the shades of the first Apaches might still dwell.

And if he saw any ghosts in the shadows thrown by the

twin fires, they belonged to his memory. To whitemen.

They belonged to Luke Masters.

And Fargo.

And Cotton.

And Jude.

And those kind of ghosts could be laid. Not easily, perhaps, for that would need time and careful planning. But bloodily. And finally.

He swallowed the last of the prairie chicken and went over to the bed of branches and grass spread along the terrace. He stretched out with his head resting on his saddle and the familiar bulk of the Winchester close to his lean body. For a while he stared up at the moon, thinking. Then he closed his eyes and went instantly asleep.

The thought that had been in his mind as he closed his eyes returned when he opened them on a high, bright day. It stayed in his mind as he cooked one of the rabbits and checked out the grey horse. It was still with him as he washed in the stream, and as he checked his traps for fresh game.

It was a thought that had not a single dimension, but many facets. If there was one single direction to it, that was that he would go back to Mattock to find Luke Masters and Fargo and Cotton and Jude.

That was the sure part. The definite part. As certain as knowing that when he opened his eyes the next morning the sun would be lighting the day.

There was no doubt about that.

The facets – the difficult part – was how.

He exercised himself and the stallion thinking about it. And gradually a pattern coalesced.

It was like planning a raid with the Chiricahua: the war-leaders and the shaman and the warriors seated about the council fire, exchanging views, arguing, putting up plans. Only this time – like so many times before – he was alone. So all the arguments, all the proposals and counter proposals, came from the facets of his own mind.

Luke Masters was the son of Jonas Masters, who owned the Box M ranch. And that meant they owned Mattock – meant that people in Mattock did what the Masters told them. Like Luke had said: they made the rules.

Fargo and Cotton and Jude were Box M hands. But closer to Luke than to his father.

Con Taggart didn't seem to like Luke much, but he wasn't prepared to chance his job bucking the rancher's son.

So: riding straight into Mattock was inviting a fresh run-in with the sheriff. Maybe a spell in jail. Maybe a hanging, or a shooting.

So: the thing was to get Luke and the others alone. Somewhere – or somehow – the four-on-one equation got cancelled out.

The problem was how.

He slept on it, and came up with the answer in the morning. At least it was a kind of answer, or maybe the first step towards an answer. He decided that he needed first to scout his killing ground, to assess the numbers and the position. To check the ground before moving in.

And soon: while the cold fury still burned inside him.

He saddled the grey after eating the last of the rabbit, then rode out through the maze of ravines and dry washes that marked the eastern edge of the mountain. He moved at a steady pace, hoarding the stallion's energy in case it was needed for a fast escape. Or a swift attack. He had no clear idea how far the boundaries of the Box M extended, but from what he had heard in Mattock it was a big spread, and he was wary of running into cowhands who might share their bosses' hatred of halfbreeds.

He met no one that day, though the next he saw three riders a long way off. On the third day, around mid-morning, he came in sight of Mattock.

He skirted round the town, moving south and east in the direction of the Masters' ranch. It took most of the day before he found clear identification of his destination in the form of a post set up beside a rutted track. The

34

post was set high enough that a man on horseback could read the words burned into the board at the top : *Box M Ranch. No Trespassers.* He turned away from the track into a stand of cottonwoods and began to ride parallel to the trail.

The ranch was built on a low knoll that occupied the centre of a shallow depression. Rolling hummocks of scrubby grassland swung in a circle about the knoll, wooded in places with stands of low, wind-torn cottonwood, but mostly dotted with cholla and saguarro. The knoll was covered with thicker grass, patterned with fences that formed a series of stock pens in which beefy seed bulls or prime breeding heifers cropped placidly. Partway up there was a fence running round the entire circumference, the in-going trail passing through a big gate with the Box M brand set large on a slab of timber hung from chains.

The ranch building itself was a low adobe structure with a second level of wood. There was a balcony running round all four sides, commanding an uninterrupted view of the land. Separate from the main house there was a bunkhouse, then a smithy and a sprawl of sheds that he guessed held tack and fodder. There was a stable close to the main building, and a barn that held wagons.

There was a man at the gate, carrying a Winchester carbine. And two more on the balcony, pacing round the building with their eyes scanning the surrounding country.

Breed watched the place until darkness settled without spotting Luke or any of the others, then turned back towards Mattock.

It was full dark by the time he reached the town, lights shining like beacons over the flatlands. There was the faint sound of a jangling piano, and the louder shouting of men, occasionally broken by the laughter of women. The moon was waned now, shaded down to a thin sliver of silvery light so that the land was shrouded in darkness. He rode in close before dismounting and leaving the grey hitched to a big saguarro that overhung

35

a shallow draw a few hundred yards from the outskirts.

He paused, thinking about the best way to find Luke Masters.

A few moments later he was drifting into the place like a prowling cat: unseen and silent, slipping through the shadows with no more sound than a faint rustling to mark his passage.

He came to the rear of the hotel and sidled down the flanking alley. There was a window opening into the tiny office behind the reception desk, pale yellow light making the shadows in the alley darker as it shone out against the facing wall. Breed eased silently onto the boardwalk and peered in. The office was empty, a deep, cloth-covered chair shoved back from a small desk with a coffee pot, a mug, and a half-finished bottle of whisky on the surface alongside a dog-eared book. The window was open. He lifted himself over the sill.

The office smelt faintly musty. There were shelves on one wall, supporting dusty ledgers, and a big safe in the corner. The outer door was slightly ajar, letting in a murmur of voices. Breed flattened against the wall, waiting.

The door swung open and the clerk came in. He was wearing the same striped pants and vest, but his shirt was white, and now the tie was fastened under his collar with a gold stickpin. The bruising under his eye was mostly gone, helped by a whitish powdering that might have been just flour. He paused with his back to Breed and tilted the whisky bottle over the mug. Lifted the mug to his mouth.

Breed waited until he had swallowed the liquor and sighed, then cupped his left hand over the clerk's mouth as his right pressed the muzzle of the Colt's Frontier against the man's cheek.

The clerk gasped and froze, his body going rigid.

'Don't make any noise.' Breed's voice was soft. 'There's no need to get hurt.'

The triple click of the hammer going back emphasised

his words. The clerk grunted something that sounded like *Urmph* and might have been *Yeah*. Breed lowered his left hand. Reached for the bottle with the Colt still tight against the clerk's face, and refilled the mug.

'Sit down,' he murmured. 'Have a drink.'

He pushed the clerk away, letting the man see the pistol. The clerk stared at it, his eyes seemingly connected to the muzzle by some invisible thread of concentration. He sat down. He picked up the mug. Drank.

'The bell still work?' Breed asked.

The clerk nodded and the tall man with the discoloured face eased the door almost shut.

'Have a drink,' he repeated.

The clerk emptied the mug in one long gulp.

'What's your name?' Breed asked.

'Levi Brown.' The words came out in a rush almost as fast as the paling of the clerk's face. 'Who're you?'

Breed stepped closer to the desk, so that the light from the kerosene lantern shone on his face.

'Christ!' said the clerk. 'You!'

'Yeah,' said Breed. 'Luke Masters caught up with me.'

The clerk touched his own face. His fingers came away with a faint dusting of white powder covering the tips. He reached for the whisky bottle and poured himself a measure.

'Bastard!'

'Him?' asked Breed, quietly. 'Or me?'

Levi Brown swallowed whisky and said, 'You was ready to pay for the room. Luke's men beat me.'

'Fargo?' asked Breed. 'With Jude and Cotton?'

Brown nodded: 'Damn' right. Bastards!'

He poured more whisky and held the mug towards Breed. The blond-haired man shook his head. Brown shrugged and emptied most of it.

'Why'd you come back?' he asked. 'They been boastin' how they run you out. They find you, they'll kill you.'

Breed smiled: 'Maybe. Maybe not.'

Comprehension dawned on Levi Brown and his eyes

got wide as his mouth gaped open.

'You come back for them,' he gasped. 'Didn't you?'

'Where would I find him?' asked Breed. 'Him an' them?'

Brown's amazement got lost behind a smile. He poured more whisky. Took a sip this time, and said : 'Fargo an' the others will be in the saloon, or Annie's whorehouse. Luke'll be either in the saloon, or down to Caleb's.'

'Where's that?' Breed demanded. 'Who's Caleb?'

Brown chuckled. 'Oh, Jesus! this is rich. Ain't no-one ever come back to pay that bastard off.'

'Where?' Breed repeated.

'Caleb's?' said the clerk. 'The hardware store. They got a place behind. Caleb and Sarah.'

Breed remembered the fair-haired girl who had smiled at him and told Luke Masters not to make trouble.

'Caleb Black,' said the clerk. 'He owns the hardware store. Runs it with Sarah. She's his daughter. Caleb'll be in the saloon now. Celebratin', I guess.'

Breed eased the hammer of the Colt down and holstered the gun. Levi Brown was radiating a feeling of hate that was almost physically tangible when he spoke of Luke Masters : the halfbreed got the feeling he could trust the clerk not to give him away.

'Why?' he asked.

'You seen Sarah?' Brown grinned lasciviously. 'Best lookin' woman in the territory. Best I seen in three years. An' not married. Not even given herself, though enough tried.'

He paused, chuckling. Breed lifted the bottle and poured more whisky. Levi Brown raised the mug – still chuckling – and drank some more.

'Caleb Black is about the only man who ain't sold out to old Jonas Masters,' he said. 'He's kept that goddam store runnin' from when all he had was a wagon loaded up with hardware. His wife got killed when a bunch of Yankees raided down during the War, an' after that he raised Sarah on his own. He won't sell out to Jonas, an' Jonas needs his goods. Luke needs Sarah the same way, only she ain't exactly selling.'

He drank more whisky and burst into a fresh set of husky chuckles.

'Luke fancies Sarah the same way a bronco stallion fancies a mare. The bastard's on heat for her. Trouble is, Sarah don't fancy him the same way. Word has it, she favours Con Taggart.'

'The sheriff,' said Breed. 'That right?'

'Yeah,' said Levi Brown. 'Poor Con's caught like a fish on two hooks. He wants Sarah an' he wants his job. He knows that if he gets Sarah, he loses his office, on account of Luke will put a word to his poppa an' get Con turned down come the October elections. So Sarah's been playing them off, one against the other. Jonas wants the marriage, because that way he buys into the hardware business an' ends up owning all of Mattock.

'If Sarah marries Con, then Jonas is gonna drive him out the same way Luke got rid of you. If she picks Luke, then Con's gonna be real mad.'

He chuckled some more and swallowed the last of the whisky.

'Feller,' he said, 'you might just decide them. Finally.'

'When I know where they are,' said Breed. 'When I know you'll keep your mouth shut.'

Levi Brown went on chuckling. 'The house is back of the store, like I said. Chances are Luke will be there right now. Hell! he spent most of today announcing his intentions. An' don't worry about me.' He touched his face again. 'I got reason enough to want Luke dead. I ain't about to give you away.'

'No,' said Breed. 'Not for two reasons.'

'Two?' Levi Brown shrugged and frowned. 'How come two?'

'If I get caught,' said Breed, his mouth curving in a wintery smile, 'I'll say who sent me. If anyone tries to catch me, I'll come back and kill you.'

The clerk went pale again as the laughter quit his face.

'I ain't gonna tell no one,' he said. 'I swear it. Jesus!

39

I got no quarrel with you. Just with Luke, for what he had done to me.'

'Remember that,' Breed said softly. 'Remember I'll come back for you if I have to.'

Levi Brown went on nodding long after the halfbreed was gone through the window and lost in the shadows of the alley.

He sat there staring at the empty whisky bottle and touching his blackened eye until a guest rang the punch-bell on the outer desk and he went out to find the room key.

The guest was a drummer selling imported whisky to saloons in the major western towns. It got sold as pure Scotch, but the drummer and the people who ran the saloons knew that it was merely laced with a measure – a small measure – of the real thing. The rest was a mixture of the cheapest liquor available that might approximate a taste of the original product. Most of it was made up and bottled in New Orleans, where fancy labels were stuck onto the bottles. After that, it got shipped out to any place the drummer could find to buy it. Mattock was one stop on a long hook from Baton Rouge to San Francisco.

The drummer's name was Hamish McCartney. He was genuinely Scottish, and when he saw Levi Brown's face he said, 'Man, you look like you need a drink.'

Brown nodded, and McCartney opened his bag to produce the real product of Scotland.

Brown swallowed two measures from the silver cup McCartney offered him, and then refused the answers to the drummer's questions.

That was the night that became known as 'The Murder'.

Years after, Hamish McCartney was still telling stories about the shooting, and how he knew the participants. The stories sold whisky very well.

Levi Brown wrote a book about it. It exaggerated the facts and obscured the reasons so that only a cloudy picture of the truth emerged. Levi made a lot of money out of the book, but at least it took the story farther on than the account of the Scottish whisky peddler. And it made Levi a lot of money; enough that he could quit clerking and live off the proceeds. Until he drank himself to death in a beat-up Missouri hotel.

What he told didn't necessarily relate to the truth, because he wasn't there when it happened.

Breed was, but he didn't make anything out of it at all.

FIVE

'Five days! Five goddam days!'

Jonas Masters palmed his chair across the room to the table that carried the liquor. He poured himself a large shot of bourbon and took a deep sip before he swung the chair around so that he faced his son again.

'You beat up on some goddam halfbreed? An' then you needed time to recover? Shit! You was off whoring. You stupid bastard.'

'I was down to Valverde, Pa,' said Luke Masters. 'I didn't think you'd need me.'

'I don't,' said Jonas. 'Not to run this place. Not so long as I'm alive. But Jesus, Luke! What happens after? You can't run a ranch like this when you're off chasin' tail every other week.'

Luke fumbled with his hat, his face turned down towards the floor. He could feel his ears getting hot as the flush spread over his face, and at the same time, feel the anger mounting.

'What you want me to do?' he asked. 'Get married?'

'Good idea,' said his father. 'Why not? Get some decent girl an' put a baby in her. At least that way we'd know that Masters will still own the Box M.'

'Who?' asked Luke, sullenly. 'You got anyone in mind?'

'Sarah Black,' said his father. 'She's overdue for weddin', an' her poppa's got a good business going.'

'That you'd like to own?' said Luke. 'That the reason?'

'Christ!' The silver-haired man tossed off the bourbon and wheeled his chair back to the table to pour a fresh measure. 'She's the finest lookin' woman this side o' San Antonio. I know you been sniffin' round there, so what's the problem? Con Taggart?'

'Partly,' admitted Luke. 'Sarah's got a shine to him.'

'He don't drink as much as you,' said Jonas. 'An' he don't frequent the whorehouse as often. But nor does he have what you got. Most he'll ever make is a Federal Marshal's pay, an' that ain't even close on what you can offer her.'

'You want me to marry her?' asked Luke. 'Just like that?'

'She's ready for children,' said Jonas. 'She's a good-lookin' girl, and her poppa owns a good store.'

'So I should wed her?' asked Luke. 'Because you say so?'

'Depends on you, son,' said Jonas. 'I want grand-children to take over this place. I don't want some Mex whore bringin' her offspring in, claiming they got a right to the Box M. I didn't build this place up for that.'

'All right,' Luke said. 'I'll do it. I'll marry her.'

'I thought you might,' said Jonas. 'Once I explained it to you.'

Luke fetched his horse from the corral, then shouted for Fargo and Cotton and Jude to join him. They rode into town together and spent the day getting ready for the proposal: getting drunk.

Luke got a shave and a haircut, then sobered up in a bath in the hotel. After that, he got kitted out in a new suit and a clean shirt. Then drank some more whisky while Fargo and the others stopped anyone from laughing at him and went down to the Mexican woman's place to beg some flowers.

He went into the hardware store with his new suit buttoned up and his neck chafing against the collar of his new shirt.

'Luke?' said Caleb Black. 'You look awful formal.'

'Come to speak with Sarah,' said Luke. 'Alone, if that's all right with you.'

'She ain't here right now.' Caleb scratched at his thin hair. 'Con Taggart took her ridin' this afternoon. Should be back soon, though, so sit a while. Have some coffee.'

Luke shook his head. He looked at the flowers in his hand and felt stupid. He dropped the bouquet on the counter where Caleb stored his guns.

'I'll be back,' he said. 'Tell her that. It's important.'

'Sure,' said Caleb. 'I'll tell her.'

Luke quit the store feeling embarrassed by his new suit. He went back to the Lucky Lady and drank some more whisky. He set up a series of watchers outside the saloon, and when Cotton came running back inside to tell him that the sheriff and Sarah were riding down Mainstreet in a rented buggy he went outside to watch.

He saw them wheel round to the stable, then watched Con Taggart hold Sarah's elbow as the peace officer walked the girl back to the hardware store. When they disappeared into the alley leading to the house he went back into the saloon and drank some more whisky.

It was dark before he set out towards the Black place, and by then he was well drunk.

Breed was crouched under the shade of a cottonwood fronting the Black home. The house was a single storey cabin of adobe and wood, a white-painted picket fence out front surrounding an attempt at a flower garden that wasn't succeeding. There was a dying tree spreading withered limbs over the remnants of the flowers, and a lean-ribbed cat doing its best to kill what remained. Luke Masters kicked the cat out of his way and hammered on the door.

Breed watched it open, lighting up the face of a tall, thin man with a bald scalp sprouting thin reminders of hair over his ears. He watched the balding man usher Luke into the house, and watched the door close.

After a while the thin man came out, saying something to Sarah as he forced the door shut against her argument. He was wearing a hat now, a wide black stetson that matched the coat covering his angular frame. He buttoned the jacket over his shirt as he paced down the

44

dying garden and settled his string tie closer about his neck.

Breed watched him go into Mainstreet, turning in the direction of the saloon.

Then the halfbreed darted out from the shadows and powered over the fence surrounding the house. He landed on his left shoulder in a flower bed, the plants making little soggy sounds as they crushed under his weight and he rolled to his feet, trampling down more blooms as he moved up to the front windows. He pressed his ear to the glass, hearing the faint sounds of voices; a door closing on receding footsteps.

He moved around the house until he thought he was level with the kitchen.

The voices were louder here.

Arguing.

And there were three.

He was about to go in when the sharp *crack!* of a pocket gun split the night air, followed by the groan of a man in pain. The detonation of the second barrel of the Derringer. And the sound of a body falling hard and dead against the bare planks of the kitchen.

Feet thudded on the planks as Breed slammed in through the door.

Luke Masters was spread on the floor like a corpse laid out for burial. His suit was black and his shirt was white. He had a string tie around his collar. And a big, red hole in his chest. The hole was made up of two close-spaced shots that had gone into his vest and torn his heart apart. There were thin red lines running from his nostrils and mouth, and his eyes were wide open, looking up at a ceiling he could no longer see.

Sarah Black looked at the halfbreed and dropped the Derringer as her mouth opened and a great tearing scream came out.

Breed crossed the room in a single movement, slapping his hand over the girl's mouth as his weight carried her down to the floor.

45

'Close it !' He grunted. 'Now.'

'And you,' said a voice that he recognised from his past.

And he cursed as a hard, heavy weight landed against his skull.

SIX

The cell was four paces wide by four across. The floor was hard-packed dirt, the walls sun-baked adobe with cement filling the cracks. The roof was corrugated metal sheeting that was bolted into the brickwork. There was a small window at the rear, set with half-inch thick bars that matched the cage at the front. There was a wooden bunk with a dirty blanket and a dirty pillow, a tin pot under the bunk. A spider had a web going in one corner, a dusty web that was heavy with the bodies of flies.

Breed opened his eyes and watched the spider extend the web by three fresh strands. It was a big, fat spider with a mottled grey body and long, delicate legs. It scuttled into the shadows as he sat up, clutching his head. There was a big, painful bump on the back of his skull. It felt hot when he touched it, and the touch sent waves of nausea spinning through his brain. He closed his eyes until the spinning sensation ended, then opened them again; cautiously.

There was sunlight coming in through the window. making patterns on the floor so that the cockroaches darted from light to shade and back again. His mouth was dry and his stomach empty. He looked at his moccasins : the throwing knife was gone. When he checked his waist, he saw that his gunbelt was missing, too. He stood up, holding his head, and went to the door. Through the bars he could see a narrow corridor running between the cells and a stone wall with a wooden door set at the centre. There was the smell of coffee.

He rattled the bars and shouted.

After a while the door opened and Con Taggart came through. The peace officer was wearing a blue shirt and faded Levis with a gunbelt on his waist. His hair and moustache were freshly trimmed. He looked neat and professional, the star pinned to his shirt gleaming brighter than the first time Breed had seen it.

'You're awake,' he said, unnecessarily. 'Thought maybe I'd hit you too hard.'

'What am I doing here?'

As he said it, Breed realised it was a foolish question. The thought was confirmed by Taggart's laugh.

'What the hell you think?' asked the sheriff. 'Waitin' for the circuit judge to come round an' find you guilty of murder an' attempted rape. You best hope he comes fast, or Jonas Masters is gonna haul you out an' lynch you.'

'Who'd I kill?' demanded Breed, clutching the bars as his head spun round.

'Christ!' Taggart shook his head. 'You sure as hell got gall, I hafta grant you that.'

'Who?' repeated Breed.

'You want it spelled out?' Taggart stroked his moustache. 'I'll tell you what I put in my report. I heard gunfire, and Sarah screaming. I entered the house and found Luke Masters dead with two .41 calibre Derringer slugs in his chest. You was down on the floor on top of Sarah. Her dress was ripped an' you was holding a Remington pocket gun. I clubbed you. Sarah says you burst in an' jumped on her.'

'I never used a Derringer,' said Breed. 'I was waiting for Luke when I saw him go in the house. I heard shots, and went through the door. The girl was holding the gun. There was someone else in there – I heard them.'

'Sure,' said Taggart. 'Pity Sarah don't back that. Way she tells it, you gunned Luke an' jumped on her. What I found was you an' a gun an' a dead man. That makes you a killer. Tough, ain't it?'

'Lies,' said Breed. 'All of it.'

'I told you not to come back.' Taggart shrugged. 'You should've listened. Now you're gonna hang.'

'Just like that?' said Breed.

'After a fair trial,' replied the lawman. And grinned: 'I'll make sure the gallows works right. I like to do things proper.'

There was an open area behind the jail. A two-hundred yard square of sandy ground with scrubby cottonwoods forming a windbreak to the south. Children played there every day, casting surreptitious glances at the window of the cell where the notorious halfbreed killer waited for his hanging. After a while the children's attention got taken up by the building of the gallows. It was a long process: two men appeared early one morning and began to off-load timber from a high-sided wagon. They set up trestles and began to saw wood. Three more appeared and began to dig holes where one of the first men had set marker posts. The holes were for the uprights of a platform that gradually took shape like a miniature stage. It was about fifteen feet by twelve, with a trapdoor at the centre. When it was finished, two long uprights were sunk down either side of the trapdoor, topped by a crossbar. The centre part of the crossbar was grooved to accommodate a rope, and a big metal hook was fixed into the platform behind the scaffold.

It took a little over two weeks before the structure was ready, and then Con Taggart and a man in a black suit supervised the fixing of the rope. It was a length of oiled hemp, looped at one end into a hangman's knot. It was passed over the crossbar and wound loosely round three times before the lower end was tied into the hook. The noose hung down far enough that it touched the planks of the trapdoor. The man in the black suit tied a weighted bag to the noose and jerked the lever that opened the trapdoor. The trap swung down, letting the bag drop. The rope stretched out, coming to a jerking stop as it extended to its full length.

The watching crowd gasped, and the man in the black suit unfastened the bag and nodded to Con Taggart.

49

His words came distantly to Breed: 'Real nice. Three feet still to go. That'll be enough so that everyone can see him. Should bust his neck the first time. If not, it'll be a few minutes afore he chokes.'

Taggart nodded and turned to look towards the jail. He grinned when he saw Breed's face, and waved.

The trial took place two weeks later.

The judge was a short, fat man in a brown suit. He wore gold-frame spectacles, and mopped his face constantly with a dark blue handkerchief. The dining room of the hotel was chosen for the court's site. The judge and Con Taggart occupied the topmost table. Jonas Masters sat in his wheelchair directly down from the judge. Breed was shackled at wrists and ankles. Sarah Black was called in as a witness.

Taggart read out a statement that followed what he had said to Breed, then Sarah was called to speak.

'He just burst in,' she said. 'I don't know where he came from. Luke had asked me to marry him, and I said "no". Then the kitchen door opened and there was firing. Shooting. Luke fell down and the halfbreed grabbed me.'

Levi Brown said: 'He broke into the hotel. He held a gun on me an' said he'd kill me if I didn't say where Luke was that night. I had to tell him, because he said he'd kill me if I didn't. Said he'd kill me if I gave him away.'

Fargo and Cotton and Jude said that the halfbreed had picked a fight with Luke Masters in the Lucky Lady saloon. Had threatened to kill Luke, and might have done so if Sheriff Taggart had not intervened.

Con Taggart said: 'I warned him off. I told him he wasn't welcome in Mattock, an' I was posting him out. I saw him clear of town an' warned him again. I thought he'd taken the warning. Until I found him trying to rape Miss Black.'

The judge asked if the defendant had anything to say.

'Luke Masters told me Mattock didn't like halfbreeds,' he said. 'He told me he'd kill me if I stayed around. He might have tried in the saloon – he was backed by those three – but the sheriff came in.'

'And that meant you had to come back?' asked the judge. 'Why?'

'Why not?' asked Breed in return. 'I've got money. Why shouldn't I?'

'This don't help the court,' said the judge. 'What reason did you have for coming back?'

'I don't like being run out of places,' said Breed. 'Do you?'

The judge hammered his gavel against the desk.

'Irrelevant,' he said. 'Give me yore version of what happened.'

Breed gave it.

The court got quiet as the judge looked at his notes.

'So,' he said, 'the accused was found on top of the woman, a corpse beside him. He had been warned to stay clear of the town, but came back. There was a gun in his hand. And he was known to have threatened the deceased with murder.

'All right. I find him guilty.'

The sentence was arranged to be carried out the following day, at noon. Breed was taken back to his cell while riders went out to alert the ranches and homesteads in the proximity of Mattock that tomorrow was the big day.

Breed got taken back and given a meal – the best he had eaten since Taggart threw him in jail.

'You know I didn't do it,' he said. 'Don't you?'

Taggart shrugged. 'That matter much now? You're gonna hang at noon. That's decided. Legally.'

'Legally,' said Breed; bitterly. 'No questions asked.'

'Like what?' Taggart said.

'Like who really killed Luke Masters,' Breed answered. 'The girl? Or you?'

Taggart laughed. 'Don't matter much now, does it?

Luke's dead, an' you're named for it. Gonna swing for it. Enjoy yore dinner.'

He went back to the outer office. The door swung shut and the lock clicked closed. The cell got quiet. Breed looked at his food. There was a big steak and a pile of mashed potato; a slice of apple pie; a pot of coffee and a mug. He began to eat.

The sun went down and the cell got dark. Taggart came in to light the solitary lantern in the corridor. He collected Breed's plates and grinned as he backed into the outer office.

'Sleep well.'

Breed slumped on the bunk, watching the fading light play over the spider's web. A moth drifted in through the window, whirring wings carrying it towards the deadly light until it got distracted by the web. It swerved round to investigate the strands. And a wing caught the sticky lines. The moth fluttered furiously, each battering movement sucking it closer into the web until it was caught on feet and wings and antennae. And the spider emerged from its corner, darting over the pattern to sink mandibles into the insect's body and paralyse the moth. For a moment there was stillness, then the spider began to weave a cocoon about the corpse, leaving it ready for later eating. Leaving it waiting. Like Breed.

The faint sound of metal rattling on metal woke him.

He opened his eyes and sat up, swinging his legs from the bunk so that several cockroaches were crushed under his feet.

'Here,' said a muffled voice. 'I can't let them hang you.'

And a parcel was shoved in through the bars of the window, falling to the floor with a dull thud.

He picked it up and peered out. A figure slid along the outer wall of the jail, wrapped in a dark cloak so that it was impossible to tell the height or sex. Before he could get any kind of distinct impression, it was gone into the night, lost behind the darkness of the scudding clouds that obscured the newly-rising moon.

He opened the parcel.

The cloth that wrapped it came away easily, revealing a twin-barrelled Remington-Elliot Derringer. There were two shells in the barrels and two more in a fold of wax paper settled inside.

He dropped the two spare cartridges into the right hand pocket of his vest, and palmed the gun.

Then he went over to the front of the cell and shook the bars.

After a while, Con Taggart came through the door.

'I want water,' said Breed. 'I'm thirsty.'

Taggart laughed.

'Takes a lotta men that way,' he said. 'They either piss or drink. Guess I could fetch you something.'

'Just water,' said Breed. 'Or coffee.'

Taggart nodded and went back out. In a few moments he returned with a pitcher of water and a tin cup. He set them down on the floor outside the cell and lifted a bunch of keys from his pocket. His Colt slid clear of the holster at the same time, muzzle lifting to point at Breed's stomach.

'Back off,' he said. 'Stay careful.'

Breed moved to the rear of the cell, close by the window. He kept his hands by his side, the little hideaway gun hidden in his palm. Taggart put the key in the lock and turned it without taking his eyes off his prisoner; leaving the key in the door he shouldered the frame open. Slow and cautious, he bent down to lift the pitcher and set it inside the cell. Followed it with the cup. Breed didn't move as the door swung shut again and the key turned. Taggart eased back, holstering the Colt.

'All right,' he said. 'Come get it.'

Breed moved across the cell. He squatted down, reaching for the pitcher with his left hand.

'What's wrong?' Taggart frowned as he began to sense

danger. 'What you got there?'

'This,' said Breed.

And his right arm thrust out through the bars, the Derringer dropping into position, trigger tight against his forefinger, the hammer against his thumb. The hammer made a loud *click!* as it snapped back.

The lawman's eyes got wide, and his frown turned into a look of outrage. His right hand dropped to the butt of his Colt.

'Don't,' said Breed, his voice sharp and clear. 'I can't miss. Not at this range.'

Taggart's hand came slowly clear of the Colt. Breed stood up.

'Open the door. Use your left hand.'

Taggart did as he was told. The door swung open again and the half-breed stepped out into the corridor. He pressed the Remington-Elliot up against the muscle of Taggart's stomach and reached over to draw the peace officer's pistol. He thumbed back the hammer of the Colt and transferred it to his right hand, dropping the Derringer into a vest pocket.

'You're crazy,' Taggart said. 'You'll never get away with this.'

'So far, so good,' rasped Breed. 'Don't try anything.'

He backed the sheriff out into the office and retrieved his weapons, replacing Taggart's gun with the more familiar weight of his own Colt. There was a clock mounted on one wall of the office : the hands stood at eleven minutes past three. Outside, the street was quiet, no light coming in through the windows.

'What you do with my saddlebags?'

Taggart's glance indicated their position behind the desk. Breed lifted them clear, then picked up his rifle from the rack beside the clock.

'Where's my horse?'

'In the stable.' A fine beading of sweat was running down the lawman's face, making his luxuriant moustache damp. 'The saddle, too.'

54

'Good,' said Breed. 'Let's go.'

He dropped the Colt's hammer and slid the pistol into the holster. Taggart took a step forwards, then halted as the Winchester slapped into Breed's right hand and the lever snapped down and up to pump a shell into the breech.

'Where you keep your horse?' he asked.

'The stable.' Taggart's voice was beginning to get ragged. 'Why?'

Breed grinned. 'You're coming with me. You got some questions to answer.'

He picked up the sheriff's gun and ejected the shells, then tossed the pistol back to Taggart.

'We meet anyone, you best have a good excuse.'

Taggart nodded and followed the prompting of the Winchester out of the office onto the silent sidewalk.

Mattock was locked up for the night. The stores and the houses were shuttered and dark, even the brothel was showing only a single red light on the door. The moon was hidden behind a fret of clouds and the air carried a faint threat of rain. An ugly white dog snarled irritably from under the sidewalk, but that was the only sound they heard as they walked fast to the stable.

Breed kept the Winchester pointed at Taggart as the lawman saddled the two horses.

'I'll be missed come morning,' he warned. 'There'll be a posse out after you.'

'After us,' Breed corrected. 'Anything happens to me, it happens to you. Remember that.'

He went out on the west side of the town, riding for close on a mile before turning north along the downward flank of the mountains. After a while he circled back, confusing the trail as he rode over hard stands of dry rock and along the beds of narrow streams. By the time the sun came up he was about ten miles from the settlement, close to a long spur of the Guadalupes that stuck like a pointing finger back the way he had come. There

55

was a gully dotted with cottonwoods and wild oaks and saguarro. He halted there and motioned for Taggart to dismount.

The sun was rising over the eastern horizon to spread pale light through the misty grey of the dawn, shafting yellow lances of light up through the clouds while the farther perimeter of the sky grew silver, then blue. Birds were singing, and as the air got warmer the cicadas began to chirrup; a coyote howled, its cry cutting abruptly off as though the light terminated its adoration of the night.

Breed stood, watching Taggart.

The lawman was rubbing his hands together as he fought the last of the dawn chill and his own fear. Dew and sweat beaded his moustache, and his eyes were suddenly hollowed by deep shadows.

'You're scared,' said the halfbreed. 'Want to tell me now?'

Taggart dragged a hand over his moustache and wiped it on his shirt.

'Tell you what?'

'Who killed Luke Masters?'

'You,' answered Taggart; stubbornly. 'Like the judge said.'

'You know that's not true,' said Breed. 'You've known that all along.'

'I'm the sheriff,' said Taggart. 'Not the judge. The judge said you was guilty. They'll be lookin' for you by now.'

'They won't find me,' said Breed. 'Not in time for you.'

Taggart did his best to sneer. 'You ain't gonna kill me. Not now. Not me bein' a peace officer. You know what that could get you?'

'Sure.' Breed chuckled. 'A hanging. So what's new?'

Realisation brought a fresh beading of sweat to Taggart's face. He stamped his feet and rubbed his hands on the legs of his denims. His tongue came out to lick at his lips. He spat a loose strand of moustache onto the ground.

'Go to hell,' he said. 'I ain't tellin' you nothing.'

Breed went over to him and swung the Winchester in a low, flat arc that drove the stock deep into Taggart's belly. The peace officer groaned and doubled over. He went down on his knees, clutching at the pain in his gut. Breed rammed the gun a second time against his belly, then landed the flat against the side of the man's face.

Taggart groaned and pitched over. While he was still on the ground Breed fetched a rope from his saddle. He checked the noose and tossed it over the limb of a cottonwood. Then he walked Taggart's horse over to a point directly under the low-flung branch and hitched the reins to the bole. He grabbed Taggart's collar and hauled the lawman onto his feet, leading him at a stumbling run to where the pony stood.

The noose settled around Taggart's neck and the man stopped groaning as it tightened. Breed heaved him bodily into the saddle and snatched the reins loose from the tree. The tail end of the rope was fastened to the trunk; about a foot of slack hung down behind the sheriff.

'Oh, Christ!' said Taggart. 'You ain't gonna hang me?'

'Who killed Luke Masters?' Breed demanded. 'Tell me.'

'I don't know.' Taggart's fingers scrabbled at the rope. 'For God's sake! I don't know.'

Breed walked the nervous horse a few paces forwards. The slack got taken up, drawing the rope tight behind Taggart's back. The brown-haired man clamped his knees hard against the pony's flanks. Breed halted, slapping the reins against his left hand.

'You knew it wasn't me,' he grated. 'Didn't you?'

Taggart nodded as best he could. 'Oh, Jesus! Yes! Sure I knew. You weren't even in there when it happened.'

'So who did it?' snarled Breed.

'I don't know. I swear to God I don't!' The sweat came thick from the man's face now, running down his cheeks to mingle with the tears spilling from his eyes so that his handsome features seemed to dissolve behind a mask of trembling moisture. 'Honest! I don't.'

57

'Tell me what you saw,' said Breed, his voice cold and flat. 'Tell me all of it.'

'Oh, Christ!' moaned Taggart, trying to insert his fingers between the noose and his neck. 'I'd taken Sarah out ridin'. We got back an' I left her at home. I asked her to marry me, for Chrissakes! Then when I went to get a drink I heard about Luke goin' courting, so I went back. I saw you there. Then I heard the shots. I come in. An' I saw you there. Someone else went out through a window. Sarah had the gun in her hand.'

His voice tailed off and his hands dropped from the rope. He closed his eyes for an instant, then opened them, staring at the bright morning sky. He shook his head as best he could with the noose holding his throat tight, and laughed.

'She was holding a Derringer. Christ! She was holding a goddam Derringer.'

'This one?' Breed lifted the hideaway from his vest pocket, throwing the breech open to expend the shells. He tossed it to the frightened man.

Taggart caught the little pistol and nodded.

'Yeah. The same model. Maybe the same gun.' He dropped it as though the metal was burning him. 'Where the hell did you get it?'

'A present,' said Breed, softly. 'A gift from a friend who didn't want me hanged.'

'Shit!' Taggart's eyes closed again. Tears squeezed out from under the lids. 'She musta given it to you. That means she musta killed Luke.'

'No,' said Breed. 'There was someone else in there.'

'I'll find him,' said Taggart. 'You just help me down, an' I'll find him, an' clear yore name at the same time.'

'You were going to hang me.' Breed's voice was very cold now, bristly as ice frosting over a winter pond; cutting off the life beneath the water. 'You didn't ask questions then.'

Taggart opened his mouth. His hands came up to clutch at the noose. He shook his head again.

'No,' he said. 'Please. No!'

Breed looked at him, impassive as the man began to tremble. Taggart had gloated at one hanging : his. He had consigned Breed to the rope. Unthinking, except to clear the woman's name; not caring whether his prisoner was innocent or guilty, only interested in settling the affair to his own advantage.

A man has to stand by what he does, his father had told him once. *He has to make up his mind an' follow that path he chooses. If it works out wrong at the end, then he should live with it. Or die for it.*

'You'd have watched me hang,' said the halfbreed. 'And laughed.'

He jerked the reins of Taggart's horse forwards as the sentence ended.

The animal snorted and ran out from under the peace officer. Taggart's hands clutched at the mane, then slipped loose, lifting up to clutch at the rope as the noose tightened on his windpipe. His feet slipped clear of the stirrups and he slid over the pony's hindquarters, his weight yanking the rope taut from the limb of the cottonwood. His feet hung no more than six inches from the ground, toes angling down as he tried to find purchase for his body on a surface that was just that fractional difference between life and death.

The noose dug against his neck. His eyes gaped wide, bulging out from the sockets as his mouth opened and his tongue jutted out. Nails broke on the hard cord, and a dark stain covered the front of his denim pants. His face went pale, then got dark with the suffusion of blood clotting the burst vessels. It became purple as a strangled cry erupted from his parted lips, from somewhere deep inside him, like the core of his life bursting. His legs lifted up, feet pumping the empty air, then straightened as the seat of his pants grew dark with the final exhalation of his body. His hands fell clear of the rope, dropping to his sides as his body twisted round and round in the warm morning air.

Flies began to settle on the spillings of the corpse. The badge shone bright in the sun. Breed looked at it turning and smiled a hard, cold smile.

'I got people to find,' he murmured. 'I can't hang around.'

SEVEN

'God damn the bastard!'

Jonas Masters wheeled his chair over the scrubbed tiles of the ranch house floor and helped himself to more bourbon. His heavy face was flushed with rage and the rim of the decanter rattled against the glass as he poured the liquor. Across the room, Fargo fiddled with the brim of his hat, watching his boss from under hooded eyes.

'He got away!' It wasn't a question. 'He got away an' took the sheriff with him.'

Fargo nodded. 'Yeah. Sometime early this morning. The cell was unlocked an' Taggart's horse is gone along with the 'breed's.'

Masters expanded his vocabulary of curses. Fargo waited. After a while the older man ran out of words and shook his head. He cupped his glass in both hands and stared down at the amber contents. When he looked up at last, his face was set in grim lines.

'I want him.' The words came out slow and clear, fury making them very distinct. 'I want him found and brought back here. This time I'll handle the hangin' myself. Take all the men you need an' tell 'em there's a bonus in it. You bring him in, I'll pay you five hundred.'

'Right.' Fargo nodded again and went out to where Jude and Cotton were waiting. He explained the situation as they headed for the corral to saddle fresh horses.

'How many men you think we'll need?' asked Cotton. 'He could be anywhere by now.'

'Not with Taggart in tow,' said Fargo.

'Why the hell would he take the sheriff, anyway?' asked Jude. 'Make more sense to leave him. Or kill him.'

'He's a halfbreed,' grunted Fargo. 'Who the hell knows

how a halfbreed thinks?'

'Someone better,' grunted Cotton. 'If we're gonna find him.'

Fargo had been a Texas Ranger once. Before an argument with another Ranger had left the man with a .44 calibre ball from a Colt's Dragoon in his belly and Fargo had deemed it best to leave the service fast. He had been a pretty good Ranger, mainly because he enjoyed killing, but also because he had a knack for organisation. He took charge now. Calling in twenty of the Box M hands, he ordered a sweep to the south and east. The men were divided into groups of five, with instructions to scour the possible hiding places immediately adjacent to Mattock. After that, they were to swing farther out, taking in Valverde and the other towns inside a three day ride. They were to go as far as the Pecos to the south, and the Brazos to the east. If they found any sign, they were to send a rider back to the ranch while the others pushed on after the halfbreed killer.

Fargo and Cotton and Jude went north.

'I got him pegged as an Apache,' Fargo explained. 'I seen Cherry Cows wearin' those kind o' moccasins before.'

'So?' asked Jude, who had spent all of his life in Texas. 'What's that mean?'

'Means he most likely knows Arizona or New Mexico better'n here,' answered the beak-nosed man. 'Most likely he'll head that way. Seein' as how he come back after the first time, I reckon he's got hisself some hidin' place that ain't too far distant. Like up in the Guadalupes. We'll head up there, an' if we find him, then we get to keep ole man Masters' bonus to ourselves.'

They rode in to Mattock and stocked up on supplies and ammunition on the Box M account, then they had a few drinks in the Lucky Lady before moving out on a north-westerly line that took them towards the foothills of the mountains.

*　　*　　*

Breed left Con Taggart hanging from the tree. He felt no regrets about the brutal impulse that had prompted him to hang the peace officer: Taggart, after all, had been willing to watch him hang on a wrongful charge. He turned the sheriff's horse loose, leaving the animal to find its own way back to Mattock as he moved out on a circling course to the east.

Going back would be dangerous, he knew, but he still wanted to find out who had killed Luke Masters to satisfy his own sense of honour.

He also wanted to settle his score with Masters' men for the beating, and the surest way he could think of to locate them was to go to the ranch. But first, he wanted to speak with Sarah Black. To find out who the third person in the room had been.

He crossed the badlands and swung towards Mattock from a point south and east of the town.

It took Fargo and the others three days to find Con Taggart. By then the lawman's body had suffered the attentions of the scavengers that followed death every-where. Flies and ants clustered about the empty sockets where once eyes had been. The boots were gone from the feet, chewed up by coyotes and badgers. The feet them-selves were tattered pieces of stumpy bone dangling over pools of dried blood that were black with insects. Tag-gart's hands were in ribbons, and his clothing was torn away as high as an animal could jump.

Cotton threw up when he saw the corpse.

Jude said, 'Christ!'

Fargo produced a knife and cut the badge from the shirt. It was stained with blood, the bright polish begin-ning to rust.

'We'll head back,' he said; slowly. 'The bastard's on a vengeance hunt. We don't need to look for him no more.'

'How's that?' Cotton wiped vomit from his face. 'How you know that?'

'Apache does this, he just means one thing,' said Fargo. 'He's warnin' us he's coming back.'

'He ain't chancin' a visit to Mattock no more'n he's gonna come to the ranch,' argued Jude. 'That'd be crazy in any man's language.'

'Apaches is crazy,' said Fargo. 'Christ! he coulda killed Taggart any time, but he didn't. He left him hangin' here.'

'Maybe that was on account o' Taggart puttin' him in jail,' said Jude, hopefully. 'Maybe?'

'Maybe,' said Fargo, 'but I don't reckon that's all. I reckon he left us a sign.' He grinned, turning his horse around. 'Which means we can bring him to us. I reckon he wants us for that beating we give him, so all we got to do is wait.'

'I ain't sure I like that,' murmured Cotton. 'Not just waitin'.'

'Be easier at the ranch,' said Fargo. 'Or in Mattock.'

They turned back towards the town, leaving the body of Con Taggart hanging from the cottonwood like a lost memory. Or a warning.

Breed left the grey stallion haltered and muffled in a stand of wind oaks a quarter mile south of town. He went in on foot, racing over the moonlit prairie in a darting run that took him from shadow to shadow until he was directly behind the outer facings of the buildings. A dog barked, and he slumped on the dry ground, scarcely breathing, until the yapping stopped. Then he got up on his feet again and moved in. Like a big cat. Like a prowling ghost.

The rear entrance of Caleb Black's house was boarded over. Where he had first burst in, the kitchen door was nailed up with planks, a tarpaulin sheet fastened inside.

He drew the Bowie knife and eased the blade between the slats. The wood into which they were nailed was soft and old, only a slight pressure needed to lift the nails clear. He worked one plank loose and set it silently on the ground behind the house, then drove the tip of the Bowie in through the tarpaulin and slashed a triangle of material loose. Thrusting his arm in through the gap, he worked the bolt to the door clear of its sockets, then sheathed the knife.

The door opened outwards. He grasped the frame in both hands and slid it gently open, then slipped inside and eased it shut again with the same care. The kitchen was dark. Over in one corner a stove glowed faintly, providing just enough light that he could see the door leading out. Beyond it was a short corridor that led into the front room. There were three other doors opening off the sides.

His moccasins made no sound at all on the faded carpet as he gentled the first one open.

Caleb Black was inside, his night-capped head resting back on a big pillow, one arm, clad in the sleeve of a striped nightshirt, hung down to the floor. Breed swung the door back into place and turned to the next.

The opening door wafted a faint odour of perfume to his nostrils. The room was dark, curtains drawn over the single window. It held the warm scent of a woman. He eased inside, slipping the door closed behind him. As his eyes adjusted to the darkness he could make out a tumble of golden hair spread over the pillow. He paused, tensed to spring forwards, but the only sound Sarah Black made was a faint sighing and a ruffle of the sheets as she turned.

Breed checked the room with automatic caution. The bed was drawn up close to the window. Against the wall on the right there was a dressing table with frilly lace all round and a big vanity mirror. A wardrobe stood against the facing wall and beside the bed there was a small table with a washbasin and a pitcher; there was a book resting face down beside the pitcher. When he crossed to the bed, he saw that the book was a cloth-bound edition of something called *Life In The Village: a romantic tale* by someone called Loretta James.

He looked down at the sleeping woman. One bare arm was thrust out over the sheets, and in the heat of the night she had wriggled the covers clear of her legs. They were nicely shaped legs, exposed almost to the joindure where her cotton nightdress had worked up. There was a line of bruises high on the right thigh. Four small bruises, like fingers might make; matched by a single, larger mark on the inside. Where a thumb would have matched the splaying of the fingers.

The nightdress had fallen off her right shoulder, the material held in decent place only by the slight swelling of her nipple. There was a mark there, too, midway over the swell of her breast. It was a dark reddish mark, as though caused by blood being drawn to the surface of the skin. It was oval-shaped.

There was another, similar mark, on her neck, on the left side.

All the marks were old. The original suffusion of blood had congealed under the pale skin to a dark blue colour that was rimmed with yellow. Breed estimated that the bruises had been made several weeks ago. He lifted his Colt silently from the holster. Then clamped his left hand hard over Sarah Black's mouth.

The woman's eyes opened as she tried to shake her head. Breed's grip denied her movement, and she began to gag, eyes focusing on the interruption of her sleep.

Realisation brought terror. Her hands came up to scrabble at the halfbreed Chiricahua's wrists. Her nails scored lines down his arms.

Breed cocked the Colt and pressed the muzzle against her cheek. Her hands fell away.

'I want to talk to you,' said Breed; softly : deadly. 'I want you to tell me who killed Luke Masters.'

Sarah rested flat on the bed, arms cupping the sheets over her body.

Breed took his hand away from her mouth as he said, 'Don't call out. I'll kill you if you try.'

He kept the Colt tight against her face as she sat up, hauling the sheets and her descending nightdress higher and firmer over her figure.

'Where's Con?' she whispered. 'What did you do to him?'

'He's dead,' said Breed.

'You killed him?'

Breed nodded.

Then : 'I'll kill you, too.'

'They'll hunt you down,' said Sarah. 'They already got posses out after you. You'd be better off running. Jonas Masters sent most of his men looking for you. That's just for killing Luke. Now they'll want you for killing Con.'

'I didn't kill Luke,' murmured Breed. 'You know that.'

Sarah smiled and said, 'They don't. After killing Con they won't even worry. You kill me, they'll never give up.'

She was right. On the legal records he was condemned to hang for the murder of Luke Masters. If anyone found Con Taggart's body – and he thought they must in time – he would be wanted for the murder of a lawman.

He saw the problem. He also saw Sarah's smile.

'Get dressed,' he said, hard and cold. 'We're talking somewhere else.'

'I'll scream,' said the woman. 'My poppa keeps a shotgun in his room.'

'You want him dead?' asked Breed. 'The way you put it, I could die as easy for a dog as a bitch.'

Sarah opened her mouth.

It closed as the barrel of Breed's Colt landed against the side of her neck. The column of metal hit the soft flesh, digging through the cotton of her nightdress to slam against the nerves connecting her body to her brain. It was a reaction born of anger : he could have silenced her more easily, using the tricks taught him by the Apache.

Sarah gasped. Breed fastened a hand on her throat and squeezed the nerve points at the base of the slender neck.

Sarah's eyes opened wide as her mouth. Then both closed.

Breed holstered the Colt and eased the window open.

He dragged the woman from her bed and carried her over to the window. It was awkward, getting her out on his shoulder, but he made it in the end and carried her down to where the edge of the garden gave onto open prairie. He crushed some more flowers on the way, but a while later he reached his horse and threw Sarah Black over the forequarters. Then he mounted and rode off with one hand resting on the woman's firm buttocks: to hold her in place.

Sarah Black opened her eyes on a brilliant sky. There was just blue above her, devoid of clouds, empty save for the distant shapes of circling birds. She shook her head as memory returned, suddenly aware of the hot sand under her body. When she turned her face to the left, the sun hurt her eyes. She turned her head away and rolled over.

Bare arms struck warm sand, and she groaned, easing up to a sitting position.

Then gasped as she felt her buttocks hit the same invading heat.

She looked down at her body: it was naked.

Instinctively, she crossed her arms over her breasts and folded her legs to hide the hair-surrounded gap between. She looked around, eyes gaping wide in unbelieving amazement.

She was in a hollow. There was sand all round her. lifting up in ten foot walls like the sides of an enormous cup. There was no visible way in or out, only the yellow sand.

She stood up, trying to cover herself.

It was a dream, she said; inside her mind, *just a dream.* Knowing it wasn't.

She looked around. The walls were blank: sheer spaces of soft sand that sloped down in almost vertical folds. Cholla dotted the rims, spiky branches denying handholds even more savagely than the blank walls denied a path out. She looked up at the sky: it was afternoon, and the sun was hot. She was sweating. She was conscious of her hair hanging down in thick folds of heat and moisture against her neck and her back and her face. She lifted her arms clear of her body to drag the hair back, and was instantly aware of the heat striking her exposed flesh.

It was a kind of rape. She didn't know where she was, only that the sun beat against her exposed body fiercer than men's eyes. Burning into her, creating a weird sensuousness that brought moisture to the space between her legs at the same time as it dried the skin of her body. Her nipples erected and began to itch. She scratched, and was instantly embarrassed as they rose harder still. She drew her hands away and folded her hair over her shoulders. It was long enough that it covered her breasts, hiding the erected nipples, but it tickled them, too, keeping them erect.

She went over to the closest place in the wall that might afford an exit. The sand was soft and came down in thin waves when she tried to climb it, falling back around her feet and scrabbling hands. It was hot on her body, like a warm bath filled with tiny scratching fingers. She gave up after a while and went back to the centre of the hollow and began to cry.

She was very thirsty.

She only realised that when she began to lick the tears from her face, and found them salty : making her thirstier still.

She crossed her legs and cupped her arms about her knees, drawing her hair, like a shroud, about her face. Her body was exposed that way, but her tears didn't fall on her skin. Instead, they plucked little holes in the sand between her naked legs, each one digging out a tiny hole that was suddenly dark, then – just as suddenly – dried by the sun.

And a shadow fell over her, bringing relief. She looked up and saw the blond-haired halfbreed standing on the rim of the bowl.

69

He held a canteen in his right hand.

He lifted it to his mouth and took a long, slow drink. Then he corked the water bottle and said, 'You feel thirsty?'

She nodded.

She couldn't speak: her mouth was too dry.

He went away, returning with a dress she recognised as one of her own. He tossed it to her, and she dragged it around her shoulders, not bothering to fasten the buttons.

She looked at the canteen. Her tongue felt covered with unpleasant fur. Her body no longer embarrassed her: she wanted the water too bad.

He took another drink. Or it might have been faking. It didn't matter: all she could see now was the canteen; and beyond it, inside it, what it held.

'Who killed Luke Masters?' he asked. 'Tell me his name.'

She looked at the canteen and shook her head.

'I don't know.'

'You were there.' The canteen swung loose on a long rawhide strap. She could hear the water sloshing inside. 'You must know.'

'I can't tell you.' The words were forced from her by the sound of the water. 'I can't.'

'You can,' he said. 'You will.'

And he disappeared behind the rim of the bowl.

Burning day faded into twilight. She hated him then, as the immediacy of the heat was softened by the breeze that started up while the sky got red and then became dark blue. Sand drifted over the rim of the hollow as stars pricked out through the fabric of the sky like shiny needle points darting through some soft velvet material. The sun went down in a blaze of red, and for a while she was grateful for the coolness. But then the sand drove against her skin, prickling the areas burned by her exposure, entering her dress no matter how she tugged it about her body. And then the air got cold. She had known it would – people had told her how the open country would switch from heat to chill when the sun went down – but she had never experienced the transformation; never known it would – could – be so dramatic.

She crouched, shivering, at the side of the hollow, tucking her body against the eastern wall of the basin as she sought out the last heated spot left by the dying sun.

A coyote howled as the moon appeared in the velvety sky. The sound brought fresh tremblings to her body, fear warming her against the chill of the night. She pulled her knees up close against her breasts, ducking her head into the thin folds of her dress, not from the cold this time, but from pure fear.

And the smell of fresh-cooked meat came to her on the night wind. It was succulent with the greases dripping from a roasting bird. She had forgotten about hunger; until now, when it became a roaring demand in her stomach.

She licked her lips, dry tongue flicking over parched skin. The smell got stronger. She clamped her teeth together and told herself not to think about it. Not to think about food or water.

But she couldn't. She stood up and began to pace around the confines of the hollow, feeling the sand chill under her feet. It was surprisingly cold. It was odd how quickly it could change from a boiling cauldron to a frosty basin.

Then something lifted out of the darkness. For a moment it obscured the stars, flapping towards her like some primeval memory dragged up out of the depths of a nightmare. She screamed, and fell down on her back as the black shape descended over her face. Her skirt rode up and scratched at her buttocks. She lifted her hands to fight off the attacking *thing*.

And felt a blanket settle over her face.

She pulled it away and wrapped it about her body, then saw a fresh shape block out the stars on the west side of the hollow.

'Hungry?' Breed chewed on a plump leg of roasted prairie chicken as he spoke. 'Thirsty?'

He lifted the canteen again, the circular shape outlined against the brightness of the stars.

Sarah Black nodded: she didn't feel capable of speaking.

'Who shot Luke Masters?'

Breed tore the last strips of flesh from the turkey's leg and tossed the bone over the hollow. Sarah watched it land on the far rim, then swung round to face the halfbreed.

He was rinsing his mouth with water from the canteen.

'I don't know.' Even to herself the words sounded dull, clogged by thirst and disbelief. 'I can't tell you.'

'I could make you,' said Breed. 'Easily.'

'What are you doing now?' she mumbled. 'What more could you do?'

The amusement in his laughter was pure evil on her ears.

'You don't know,' he said. 'I've given you the easy way so far. I'll give you a little bit longer. Not much, because they'll find Taggart's body soon. If they haven't already. Soon I'll have to make you talk – the Apache way.'

Sarah said something her father had always told her not to say. Breed answered with a chuckle and faded over the rim of the hollow.

The night got colder and very lonely.

Morning wasn't much better. The dew she sucked off the blanket did no more than give her taste of the water she wanted. And the sight of the halfbreed chewing on the remnants of the prairie chicken set up a rumbling in her stomach that was most unladylike.

'What will you do if I tell you?' she asked. The way her mouth was dried out it sounded like *wattleu doofiyellu*.

'Take you back to Mattock,' said Breed. 'After you tell Jonas Masters.'

Her answer was suddenly distinct: 'No!'

Breed shrugged, and faded back from the rim of the hollow.

The day opened up. A big, bright sun climbed across the sky, filling the basin with heat. A lizard came down in a tiny spill of sand. Rolled for a moment with pale feet dancing on the air, then turned and lashed its tail until it was clear of the miniature landslide and could right itself again. It ran fast across the bottom of the hollow and began to ram its clawed feet against the sand on the far side.

Sarah watched it try to climb the slope.

Each time it gained purchase on the sandy bank a fresh spill of sand drifted down to roll it to the bottom. The lizard tried for a long time, but it couldn't quite handle the angle and the slippery sand.

After a while, she stood up and went over to where the tiny reptile was fighting its way clear of a fresh spill of sand.

It was green, with yellow markings that blended its body against the ground. She was surprised to find that its body was dry in her hands. It had a long tail and tiny feet that ended in little claws. The eyes were opalescent black, still as the water in a quiet pond.

She threw the lizard over the rim of the hollow and wished there was someone to pick her up in the same way.

But there wasn't. There was only the gold-haired half-breed demanding an answer.

An answer only she could give him.

She went back to the centre of the sun-washed basin and began to shout as best she could: 'All right! I'll tell you.'

Breed showed on the rim. He was holding the canteen, the plug dangling loose so that water spilled over the neck.

Sarah Black stared at the precious fluid and said again, 'I'll tell you. I swear it. But give me water first.'

Breed corked the bottle and tossed it into the hollow.

He watched as the woman grabbed it and began to gulp the tepid water.

'It's amazing,' he said, 'what people will do for a drink.'

EIGHT

Sarah Black crouched in the shade of a big saguarro, chewing on a piece of wild turkey. Breed squatted facing her, and she studied him as she ate.

His features had struck her the first time he walked into the store: a mixture of white and Indian blending into a bone structure that was almost classically handsome. She had noticed his eyes, especially when Luke had insulted him. They had seemed to freeze then, burning with a cold intensity that had sent a shiver down her spine as she realised that he was dangerous. Years before, when her mother was still alive, her father had taken them to San Antonio and bought tickets for a circus that was passing through. The main attraction had been an enormous block of pure gold, but what had stuck in Sarah's mind was the tiger. It was a magnificent beast, all muscle and controlled strength. It had radiated a feeling of danger, and when a man had rattled a stick against the bars of its cage, the animal had spun to face him, lips drawing back from great, yellow fangs as the eyes fastened on the man and a coughing roar burst from the throat. Breed reminded her of the tiger.

Now his eyes were impassive. They were neither menacing or comforting, merely calm. Waiting. In a way, it was even more unnerving than his anger. She picked the last scraps of meat from the bone and swallowed water.

Breed corked the canteen and said, 'Now tell me.'

The woman wiped her mouth, knowing that she had no other choice.

'Luke came courting,' she said. 'He'd been round before, but all he ever wanted was . . .'

'Yeah,' prompted the halfbreed, 'I know.'

'Well, anyway.' She sought for the right words, wondering if there was some way she could tell the story without revealing all the details. Not wanting to face the outcome of her revelation. 'I'd been riding with Con. He'd been visiting, too. He'd talked about us getting married, but Poppa said he didn't earn enough and, anyway, it wouldn't be much of a life, being married to a peace officer. He said that I'd do better marrying Luke, because then we'd be rich. I knew Con wouldn't leave his work, and even if I did marry him, Luke's father would make things difficult. Poppa said that Jonas would run Con out of town. Even make it hard for him to find another post. And I couldn't just leave Poppa, not on his own – he depends on me too much.'

She paused, looking down at the sand where her fingers were tracing a vague pattern.

'Go on,' said Breed.

'Well.' She wiped the pattern away, teeth nibbling at her lower lip. 'When I got back that day, Poppa was waiting. He said he wanted to talk to me, so Con went off. He said he'd come back later to get an answer. He said I had to make up my mind, because he wasn't waiting much longer.

'Poppa said that Luke had been round, saying he wanted to marry me. Poppa had given his permission, so Luke was coming back. Poppa said he'd send him over from the saloon.

'When Luke arrived, he was pretty drunk. He'd spent most of the afternoon in the Lucky Lady with those friends of his. He said he wanted to marry me. Started telling me how we'd live out on the Box M, and how he'd inherit the ranch when his father died. He said Jonas would put money into Poppa's store, and it would be the biggest hardware place in all of Texas. He said how we'd get married in San Antonio and then have a big party back in town. How Jonas would invite all the important people, and that would help Poppa's store. It was like he was trying to buy me.

'I said I couldn't marry him. I didn't love him. So then he got angry and started talking about Con. How he'd make sure Con would lose the next election. Run him out, and fix it with his father that Con wouldn't get another job. Then he kissed me. He smelt of whisky and his hands were all sweaty. I told him to stop it, but he wouldn't. He went on.'

She shuddered, lashes lowering to hide her eyes.

'He got . . . Demanding . . . He started pawing me. He tore my dress. He bruised me.'

'I saw,' said Breed.

She blushed, not meeting his gaze.

'Yes. Well, anyway, he tore my dress and tried to . . . force me. I guess Poppa was wondering what was happening, because he came back about then. Luke didn't hear him come in. Nor did I. The first I knew he was there was when he shouted. He said, "Get off her, you bastard". Luke had me on the floor, and when he heard Poppa shout, he turned around and started reaching for his gun. Poppa had that Derringer he keeps in his belt. He shot Luke. It was horrible. Luke never got his gun out. He just sort of coughed and fell back with blood coming out of his chest. I don't think Poppa knew what he was doing, really.

'But then there was a knocking on the front door. That was Con. I suppose he'd heard that Luke was visiting and come round to check. Then you came in. Poppa just lost his head. He dropped the gun and ran out. Then Con found you.'

'And you let him think I killed Masters,' said Breed. 'Or was that just an easy answer? Taggart must've seen your father.'

Sarah nodded. Slowly; wearily.

'He saw Poppa. He said that if Jonas found out Poppa had shot his son, then Poppa would hang. He said Jonas would make sure of that. He said it was better to say you did it. I'm sorry.'

'Now,' rasped Breed, and she heard the same anger in

his voice she had heard in the store and at the trial.

'I gave you the Derringer,' she said. 'I couldn't leave you to hang.'

'I might have used it on Taggart,' said Breed. 'Didn't you think of that?'

Sarah Black nodded again. 'I couldn't just leave you. I felt guilty. You killed Con anyway.'

'He knew I was innocent,' Breed grunted. 'We both knew that, but he was going to hang me, anyway. I just returned the favour.'

'Oh, God!' moaned Sarah. 'I wish you'd never come here.'

'That wouldn't have stopped Luke Masters,' said the halfbreed. 'Wouldn't have stopped you. If I hadn't been there, who would you have blamed? Taggart?'

The woman shrugged. 'I don't know. I couldn't let Poppa hang. Could I?'

Breed stared at her. Somewhere inside her mind there was a thought process that rationalised her lies and made them defensive truths. She had been protecting her father the only way she knew how, against the might of the Masters ranch. In the same circumstances he might have done the same thing. Except for one factor.

His own life was at stake.

There was something his father had told him once: *When it all boils down,* Kieron Gunn had said, *you got to look after yourself. I don't just mean staying alive, but what goes on inside you. You need to follow whatever path you think is right. You got to live with yourself. You can run from a man following you, but you can't ever run from yourself.*

He saw tears in the woman's eyes. Ignored them as he stood up and fetched the grey horse over.

'Where are we going?' she asked.

'To tell Jonas Masters,' answered Breed. 'To tell him how his son got killed.'

'No!' Her voice trembled. 'Please! I'll do anything.'

She opened her dress, easing it down over her shoulders

so that her breasts were exposed. Sunlight struck the twin mounds, angling shadows down from the nipples. She looked at him, dark lashes fluttering over grey eyes.

'Please?'

'Get dressed.' Breed saddled the horse, ignoring the stir her body roused in his. 'You got two men killed already. I'll not be the third.'

'Money?' She fastened her dress. 'Poppa would pay you.'

He belted the cinch tight and checked the stirrups. Not bothering to answer.

'You'll never make it,' she said.

'I wasn't trying,' answered Breed. 'Hadn't you noticed?'

The woman blushed, then: 'Jonas won't believe you. He'll have you killed.'

'Maybe,' said Breed. 'Maybe not. I guess it depends on how I tell the story. How you tell it, too.'

'I'll say what I said at the trial.' She stared at him with her face getting angry. 'I'll do anything to protect Poppa.'

'Yeah?' Breed grabbed her arm. 'You sure?'

He manhandled her over to the pit in the sand. From the upper level it was like a shiny, scoured bowl. The sun struck the sides and the bottom and got reflected back in a brilliant blur of light that was broken only by the prickly cactus plants around the rim.

'You want to wait there?' he asked. 'While I fetch Jonas Masters?'

Sarah Black shook her head.

'Then let's ride,' said Breed. 'My way.'

NINE

'He killed him,' said Fargo. 'Christ Jesus! He strung him up an' left him dangling. When we found him, he'd been got at by animals. There wasn't that much to take. Except this.'

He handed Con Taggart's badge to Jonas Masters.

The rancher looked at the stained shield. And Fargo anticipated the next question.

'He's part Cherry Cow, Boss. They're the meanest streak. He'll want satisfaction.'

'He won't come here,' said Jonas Masters. 'He wouldn't dare.'

Fargo shrugged. 'You remember when them fellows took young Chato's wife? He followed them through. Killed them one by one. That's how a Cherry Cow thinks: he gets hisself a grudge, he don't give up.'

'So?' asked Jonas. 'What you suggesting?'

'We wait,' said Fargo. 'Way I see it, he's got a grudge agin me an' Jude an' Cotton. That means he'll come here.'

Jonas Masters smiled. 'If he does, take him alive. I want to see him hang.'

'Right,' said Fargo. 'I'll remember that.'

The moon was filling back to a round orb as Breed approached the ranch house. It spread a pale light over the adobe of the lower buildings, and the wood that made up the higher level glowed warm in the night.

Sarah Black was with his horse, in a stand of cottonwoods. Her ankles and wrists were tied together, and there was a gag in her mouth. Breed was on foot. His hair was tied back under the leather warband of the

Chiricahua Apache, and he was armed with only his Colt and the two knives.

He got up to the fence surrounding the ranch house and slithered under the poles. A Hereford cow snorted nervously and he paced gently towards her, clasping the moist nose as she prepared to bellow and blowing into the deep funnels of her nostrils. The heifer snorted contentedly and he went past her.

There was a space between the inner circle of the corral and the house itself. He got down on his belly and began to move over the open ground like a snake. No one saw him, and he reached the side of the house and folded into the shadows under the porch.

A door opened, and he slipped inside. He was in a kind of hall, white walls leading forwards to a dark wood door. He opened the door and went into a dark room. There was a tall clock against the far wall, its sound echoing loud in the stillness. The hands of the clock both pointed vertically. A gong somewhere inside struck a single, belling note.

He crossed the floor and climbed the stairs leading up to the gallery.

A light showed from under a door.

He opened it, the Colt in his hand.

Jonas Masters looked up from the book he was reading and opened his mouth. Then shut it as Breed came into the room with the gun pointed on the old man's face.

'Don't try anything,' said Breed, moving across the carpet to the wheelchair. 'I got nothing to lose.'

Jonas folded a marker into the book and tossed the volume onto the bed. It was something called *Gunlaw* by Charles Garrett.

'You're dead,' said Masters. 'The moment you squeeze that trigger.'

'I know,' Breed replied. 'But so are you. So listen.'

'To what?' Jonas palmed his chair clear of the bed. 'To a halfbreed who killed my son?'

Breed faced the old man, the Colt levelled on the lined face.

'I didn't,' he said. 'Caleb Black shot your son.'

Jonas laughed. 'Sure, I believe you. Trouble is, the judge didn't.'

'Sarah Black is close by,' said Breed, 'She knows the real story. Listen to her.'

'Why?' Jonas shook his head. 'You killed Luke.'

'No,' said Breed. 'I didn't.'

'You got convicted,' said Masters. 'Why should I believe anything else?'

'Because,' said Breed, 'I'll kill you if you don't listen.'

'Sarah would have spoken up,' said Masters. 'Before now. At the trial.'

He ignored the threat, confident of his supremacy. Too assured of his station in life to countenance the arguments of a halfbreed Apache. Too safe in his own home – his own empire – to believe that some intruder might threaten him.

Breed lifted the pistol and pressed the muzzle against the old man's face.

'You're going to talk to Sarah,' he grated. 'You're going to listen to the truth.'

The silver-haired man ignored the gun. Where fear should have shown in his eyes there was only contempt. He chuckled.

'How the hell you think you'll fix that?' His voice was bitter. 'It takes two men to get this goddam chair downstairs. You try to carry me out, someone's gonna spot you – my boys are waitin' for you.'

'They didn't see me come in,' grunted Breed.

'They'll sure as hell see you go out,' said the old man. 'All the way.'

As he spoke, he glanced at the door. He seemed unafraid, as though the prospect of his death left him unmoved. Instead, he seemed to be waiting. And for the first time, Breed understood the full extent of his injury : Jonas Masters could no more get himself into bed than he could walk down the stairs. Yet the bed was prepared for sleep; pillows were stacked against the headboard and the covers were turned down. Masters was still dressed : he wore a dark blue shirt, and from under the blanket covering his legs, there protruded the tips of highly-polished boots. Breed realised that he *was* waiting. Realised that he needed someone to help him into bed. And was expecting that someone to arrive and give the alarm.

The clock in the room below chimed the half-hour. Masters smiled and said, 'You're dead, boy.'

'Not yet.'

Breed clamped his fingers tight about the old man's neck. The tips probed for the nerve points below the jaw, and Jonas Masters' eyes opened wide in surprise as the sudden pressure reduced his body to the same numb state as his legs. His eyes glazed over, the lids slowly closing as his head lolled to the side.

Breed stepped away from the wheelchair as a discreet knocking rang against the door.

He moved on silent feet to the wall, watching as the door swung open and a Mexican in a white tunic and *huaraches* came in with a tray. The man smiled as he saw Masters, and he began to tiptoe across the room. He set the tray down on the bed and stooped to pick up the fallen book. While he was bent over, Breed came forwards and hit him once. On the side of the neck, using the butt of the Colt. The Mexican grunted and slumped flat. Breed lifted the tray from the bed and settled the Mexican under the covers. He dragged them up to the man's chin, then shifted a pillow so that it hid most of his dark hair. Then he doused the light and stooped down to drag Jonas Masters from the wheelchair, onto his shoulder.

The old man was heavy, one hundred and seventy pounds or more, and his unconsciousness made him pure dead weight, limp as a waterlogged sack. Carrying him down the stairs was difficult.

Taking him out was harder.

Breed got him onto the porch and halted there, panting as he listened to the slow pacing of the guard on the balcony. The footsteps halted at the corner, then a muffled voice said, 'Got a light, Duke?' There was a grunt of affirmation and the guard moved round to the rear of the building. A match scraped on a striker and tiny glow of flame showed through the underpinnings of the verandah. A voice said, 'I don't know what the hell we're doin' out here. That 'breed ain't gonna risk comin' in.' And the first voice answered, 'Orders. Beats ridin' line.'

Breed tugged Jonas Masters' belt from his pants and fastened it under the man's arms. Clutching the leather in his left hand he began to ease towards the fence, dragging the old man behind him.

It was difficult getting the supine body up on the grey horse, and then he needed to lash it in place. He put Sarah Black in the saddle and ran a line under the stallion's belly, fixing her ankles to the stirrups. Then he took the reins and began to trot away from the Box M. It was hard going, but he was wary of overburdening the stallion.

He halted at dawn, somewhere south of Mattock, gagging both the woman and the old man before he rode away.

It was noon by the time he returned with two horses, a piebald mare and a roan gelding.

'Horse stealin's a hangin' offence,' grunted Masters as Breed tied him to the saddle. 'You ain't got a chance.'

Breed just laughed and led the way out on a wide-swinging circle that took them clear of the town and into the badlands beyond. He went back through the arid country north and west of Mattock, moving steadily towards the hidden canyon.

When he reached the place, he put the horses inside the corral and carried Jonas Masters up to the adobe, then he untied Sarah and helped her up the steps to the terrace.

'This is crazy,' said the old man. 'What the hell you doin' this for?'

'Like I said,' Breed's voice was cold as he answered, 'I want you to hear the truth.'

He looked at the woman. She shook her head.

'Tell him,' he said. 'Tell him what you told me.'

Sarah was abruptly reminded of the tiger again. Of the moment it turned in its cage, yellow eyes blazing, the great claws extending from the pads. She remembered that sudden explosion of movement, of raw, feral anger, when it had hurled itself across the cage. And now there were no bars separating her from the raw fury.

She told Jonas Masters what she had told Breed.

'Oh Jesus!' said the cripple. 'I never knew.'

'What'll you do to Poppa?' the woman asked.

Masters shrugged. 'Ain't much I can do. It depends on him.'

He looked at Breed as he said it, his mouth curling in distaste.

'He was guarding his daughter's honour,' said Breed. 'Why not leave him be?'

'That mean you're lettin' us go?' Masters asked. 'After I promised to hang you?'

'Why not?' Breed stared back at the old man. 'I squared things with you. You're out of it now.'

'What else you plannin'?' asked Masters. 'More murder?'

Breed shook his head. 'Murder?'

'You killed Taggart.'

'He was ready to kill me. I owed him as much.'

Within the tenets of Apache justice it was a reasonable argument: a life taken for a life threatened. That side of the halfbreed's nature that still thought in the way of his mother's people saw the logic of the argument. Not even an argument, merely a rational extension of the law – often brutal – of survival. At the same time, that part of his mind that was governed by his father's influence told him that no whiteman would see it the same way. The *pinda-lick-oyi* would kill, sure. To shoot a man wearing a gun was acceptable. It need not matter that one man – gifted with speed and skill – must inevitably kill the other; that was not murder. Not in their eyes. That was a fair fight. Unless the whiteman's law decided differently, and the killer was taken out and hung. That was fair, too – by their rules. But for a halfbreed to take a man who had tried to kill him, and do the same – exactly the same, save for the difference of parentage – that was wrong.

Jonas Masters surprised Breed by saying, 'Yeah. I guess you did.'

He looked down at his dirty pants. Touched them, kneading the withered flesh beneath, then : 'I lived with a lot of hate inside me for a long time. I guess that watchin' Luke grow up kept it alive. I raised him to hate injuns. Halfbreeds, the same. I never figgered for one to bother clearin' his name. I guess now I see how a whiteman can be just as mean. Christ ! I never figgered Luke to be so wild. Guess that's my fault : I raised him that way. Gave him everything he wanted; never questioned what he did. Maybe if I had, he'd be alive now.'

He turned towards the woman and wiped a hand across his face. The hairs on the back shone moist in the sun.

'Yore Poppa did what I'd have done. I ain't gonna say a thing about this. He's clear an' free.'

He looked at Breed.

'I can't answer for the law, but the way I see it, there ain't no real evidence you killed Con Taggart. Circumstances hafta point that way, but I'll do what I can to hush that up. Be advisable to stay clear o' Texas fer a while.'

Breed smiled : a mixture of gratitude and hatred.

'It's not finished yet,' he said.

'What you mean?' asked Masters. 'I don't understand.'

Breed touched his face. The bruises were mostly gone now, but around one eye, and on his mouth, the marks of the beating still showed.

'Luke and his men did this,' he said; quietly. 'I still have a debt to settle.'

86

'Jesus!' A flare of Jonas' old anger rose to the surface. 'Can't it end here?'

Breed shook his head. 'No. I'll take you back to Mattock. When you get there, you tell them I'm coming.'

Jonas shook his head. 'They'll kill you. Those boys are mean.'

Breed grinned. It was a cold expression.

'Just tell them I'm coming.'

He left Jonas Masters and Sarah Black a quarter-mile outside of town, then made camp in an arroyo off to the south and east. It wasn't far from the Valverde trail, where Luke Masters and Fargo and Jude and Cotton had found him that night.

CHAPTER TEN

'You're crazy!'

Fargo's voice was a nervous snarl. He plucked at the brim of his hat and stared at the old man in the wheelchair.

'Maybe,' said Jonas Masters, 'but that's what I'm telling you.'

'An' on the say-so of some goddam killer halfbreed you're lettin' us go? Just like that?'

'Just like that,' said Masters. 'You worked for my son, anyway. You never did much around here.' His gesture took in the stock pens and the fences surrounding the main ranch building. 'Now Luke's gone there ain't much reason to keep you. Here. Severance pay.'

He tossed an envelope to Fargo, who caught it neatly, fingers rustling the notes inside.

'Three hundred dollars,' said the cripple. 'Share it between you.'

'What the hell did that 'breed bastard say to you?' asked Fargo. 'To change yore mind this way?'

'Maybe he told the truth,' answered Masters. 'Or maybe he just made me see what I was. It don't matter, you just get off my land. Luke's gone now, so there ain't no one to protect you.'

'You'll be sorry,' Fargo snarled. 'You'll regret this.'

'Get out,' said Masters. 'He's waitin' for you.'

'Hundred each,' said Jude. 'That ain't bad.'

'Could've been more,' grumbled the beak-nosed man. 'If Luke hadn't got hisself killed.'

'How much we made in all?' asked Cotton.

Fargo thought for a while, then grinned. 'Close on a

thousand with this.' He tapped the envelope. 'An' we still got them cows in the south section. Shit! that goddam cripple never even knew his son was runnin' cows off his own land. Poor old bastard!'

The redhead and the youngster laughed.

'What we gonna do now?' Jude asked. 'With that halfbreed lookin' for us?'

'Spend some money,' said Fargo, laughing. 'He ain't gonna come into Mattock, so we'll wait around a bit. Have us some fun. Then we'll move them steers out an' sell 'em over towards Grantsville.'

The others joined in his laughter. They didn't know what was coming.

Breed waited long enough for Jonas and Sarah to get back home. Then he waited a day longer. After that, he went into the town. On foot, coming up behind the Black house and waiting until he was sure Sarah was alone inside.

'You meant it,' she said, surprised when he came into the kitchen. 'I didn't think you would.'

'They won't either.' He lifted a chicken wing from the pan and began to gnaw on the meat. 'That's what I counted on.'

'And me?' she asked. 'You counted on me, too?'

'You won't tell anyone.' He looked hard at her grey eyes. 'Will you?'

'I could.'

'I don't think so,' he said. 'That'd mean your father getting named as Luke's killer. Best to leave it. Best to help me.'

'How?' She wiped a strand of blonde hair back from her face. 'What do you want me to do?'

The question surprised her. She hadn't meant to ask it, but somehow it had come out. It was, she thought, partly because he had never tried to paw her, just treated her with respect. Except for when he had taken her naked to that sandpit, but even then he had not sought the kind of advantage Luke or Con had wanted. And in another part, it was gratitude for not revealing her father as Luke's killer. At least not where it counted: to the upright citizens of Mattock, who might have demanded a fresh trial. And in another part, it was – maybe – the attraction she felt. He was different. Not like anyone she had known. Not like Con or Luke; not like anyone.

She wondered what it might be like, in bed with him; or on a blanket under the open sky.

'Well?' she asked, feeling a blush suffuse her face.

He stared at her, his eyes surveying her body as if he knew what was in her mind.

'Fargo and the others? Where are they?'

'In the saloon, mostly,' she said. 'The whorehouse got a new girl, and Cotton spends most of his time with her. When he's not in the saloon.'

'When's that?'

'Cotton's there afternoons and nights.' She poured more oil over the frying chicken. 'They all seem to have a lot of money. Fargo and Jude spend more time in the saloon.'

'Thanks.' He dropped the chicken wing onto the table. 'Thanks a lot.'

After he had gone she found it hard to concentrate on cooking her father's dinner. She wanted to follow him. Wanted to see what he did. She wondered if she had fallen in love with him, then sighed and went back to the food.

It was the wildest night Mattock had experienced since the killing of Luke Masters. It brought the bordello a whole new trade of gaping, vicarious customers who wanted to see where it happened. Jonas – who owned a one third share in the place – made money out of it.

And it all happened because four men had beaten up a halfbreed.

Breed left the Black house in the early evening. The sky

was getting still and quiet as it prepared for the setting of the sun. By the time he reached his horse and rode it round to the north side of the town, the sky was dark. There was a big moon shining down, so that Mainstreet shone palely in the ethereal light. The stores were closed. The houses were either dark, or showing faint glow from behind curtains and shutters. Someone's caged bird trilled a farewell to the sun, shutting off as darkness fell.

He tethered the horse behind the brothel and studied the building. It was two storeys high, a slope-roofed verandah running round the lower level, where a porch lifted up from the raw sand of the prairie. There was no fence out back, just a line of barrels filled with empty bottles and scraps of food. There were dogs scrabbling around the scraps.

Light showed at the rear, matched dimly by fainter radiance from a few of the upper windows. The back door was open, exhaling the smell of food and liquor into the night.

He paced over to the corner and stepped onto the porch. An upright pole granted purchase enough, so that he was able to climb onto the roof. The wooden tiles were hard and dry, crackling under his feet. What sound he made was lost under the creaking of bedsprings and the groans of the clients, the feigned-pleasure moaning of the whores.

At the end of the building there was an open window giving access to a corridor running the length of the upper storey : he climbed inside.

The corridor was dark, lit only by two dim, red lamps at either end. It looked down onto a central room that held a bar at one end and a series of tables at the other. There was a woman with hennaed hair playing a piano that was backed up against a window. She was wearing a corset of striped red and black silk, and dark stockings. A man with brilliantined hair was serving drinks, and just beyond the open outer door there was a big man with a pick-haft clutched in his arms like a sceptre.

Breed paced down the corridor, checking the rooms for light. Three places down he saw a glow from under the frame and turned the handle.

A girl with frizzy brown hair sat up in bed and smiled at him. She dropped the nailfile she was using and smiled, exposing bad teeth. She had a black velvet choker round her throat and nothing else. Her breasts were small and pointed, ending in little dark nipples that were outlined with rouge.

'I didn't know you was coming, honey,' she said, 'you coulda brought a bottle.'

'I'm not,' said Breed. 'You know who Cotton uses?'

The whore pouted. 'I'm as good as Maybellene. Why you want that three to a bed stuff? Stay with me.'

He smiled and shook his head. 'Which room?'

'Two down. Didn't they tell you?'

'No,' he said. 'Thanks.'

'My pleasure. Or might have been.'

He shut the door and went on to Cotton's room.

Cotton was named for the crop his father grew back in Louisiana. His full name was Cotton Frederick Rockwell, but he thought just Cotton sounded more suitable for a gunfighter. He had run away from home when he was sixteen years old, drifting around Texas as he built himself a modest reputation as a mean kid to cross. He had worked ranches and ridden shotgun for a local stageline; played a minor part in a small range war; rustled cattle and once held up a store. Three years ago, he had met Luke Masters and joined the payroll of the Box M. Cotton was twenty-three now.

He wasn't thinking about his past as he lay back in the creaking bed and watched Maybellene's dark hair moving between his spread thighs. He wasn't thinking about anything except the moment, and the pleasure it was bringing him.

Until the door opened and the past – and what little was left of his future – came through the door.

*　　　*　　　*

Breed was holding the throwing knife flat in his right palm, his hand slightly out from his side. There was no light in the room, but the window was wide open and moon's light was coming through, bright. It illuminated Cotton's mouse-coloured hair. It shone on the buttocks of the girl between his legs.

It threw Cotton's face into stark relief as his mouth opened in a snarl and he rasped, 'What the hell? Get outta here.'

The woman pulled away, her mouth open in an expression that was part surprise and part annoyance.

Cotton recognised Breed first. The shadow across his face made it impossible to tell whether his eyes showed anger or fear, but his action was clear enough. He slammed both knees up against the woman's breasts, pitching her backwards in a kneeling position that blocked his body. He rolled on his right elbow, left hand clutching for the gunbelt hung from the bedhead. He moved fast, fingers closing on the ivory grip of the closest Remington.

Breed moved faster. His right arm flung forwards and up, hand opening to release the throwing knife. The slender blade glittered in the pale light. And then the glisten of the metal was lost in the darker colour of Cotton's hand, the even darker colour of his blood. It went in through the back, the point extending from the palm so that it dug into the leather of the gunbelt. Cotton winced in pain and instinctively yanked his hand away. The movement tore the blade through his flesh, severing tendons so that his fingers jerked rigid and were then limp, useless appendages that dripped shadow-blackened blood over his hips and belly as shock froze his reactions and he sat, staring at the dark tip protruding from his palm.

Breed went across the room almost as fast as the knife. The woman was holding her breasts and opening her mouth to scream. The halfbreed clubbed her with his bunched fist. Once, heavily, on the side of the jaw. Her mouth snapped shut and her eyes closed. He hit her again, this time on the side of the neck, using the edge of his left hand. She fell across Cotton's legs.

Her body seemed to break the trance-like spell of shock that gripped the young gunfighter. He said, 'Oh, Jesus! Oh, hell!' and kicked clear of the body and the bed, reaching for his guns with his good right hand.

Breed came over the bed with a disregard for the whore's unconscious form that left bruises on her thighs and stomach and cannoned him into Cotton. The Bowie knife flashed bright in the moonlight – there were too many people below to chance the sound of gunfire – and pressed against Cotton's throat.

The young man's hand froze on the ivory butt. He said, 'Don't. Please.'

Breed held the blade tight against his windpipe as he reached round to hike the two Remingtons clear of the bed. He tossed the belt across the room. Then he took the haft of the throwing knife and hauled it clear of Cotton's hand. Cotton moaned as the metal twisted, grating on bone. Fresh blood pulsed from the wound, trickling over his wrist.

'Turn around.' There was winter in the halfbreed's voice. 'Do it slow and quiet.'

Cotton turned. His body was pale, his eyes very wide and watery. A nervous tic had started up at the corner of his mouth.

'What you gonna do?' His voice was shaky, teetering on the verge of hysteria. 'Please, don't hurt me no more.'

Cold blue eyes studied his face with the same interest a cat shows in a wounded mouse. Breed said, 'You hurt me. You were ready to kill me.'

'Christ! that was Luke.' Urine splashed down Cotton's naked legs. 'He ordered me. I never . . .'

The words cut off as Breed's right hand moved. Twice. Almost like a slap. But where his palm might have landed there was, instead, the heavy blade of the Bowie. Two cuts appeared on Cotton's face. Above and below his lips. Blood covered his mouth and chin, began to drip onto his chest. Teeth showed momentarily through the higher slash, then were hidden behind the curtain of blood. He sobbed and went down on his knees, hands pressed against his face. Crimson dripped from between his fingers.

Breed grabbed the right wrist, dragging the arm out from the body. He hacked the Bowie down in a short, vicious arc that ended where the fingers joined the palm. The flesh parted as the razor edge cut through to the tendons, into the muscles. A great sobbing intake of breath set Cotton to choking on the blood still filling his mouth. Breed hacked again and the web of flesh between forefinger and thumb was divided down to the joint, a great spurt of scarlet jetting from the sundered veins.

Cotton's face went the colour of a fish's underbelly. He stared at his hand, then began to vomit, great wracking heaves shaking his body.

He didn't hear Breed rasp, 'Your gunfighting days are over.'

He did feel his hair grasped so that his head was tugged back, forcing him to look up at the blond-haired man standing over him. The moonlight shone on Breed's face, throwing the lean planes of his cheeks into stark relief, emphasising the feral intensity of his eyes. His mouth was set in a thin, ugly line.

'There a doctor here?' he asked.

'Yeah.' Through the severed lips it was a sibilant whistle.

'Good.' Breed let go the hair and motioned for Cotton to stand up. 'You understand me?'

'Yeah.' Cotton let himself be pushed back onto the bed.

'You know how long it takes a man to die of a belly wound?'

Cotton shook his head, sending droplets of blood spraying to either side.

'A day,' said Breed; very slow, very distinct. 'Maybe longer. Long enough for you tell the others I'll be waiting for them where you found me before. On the Valverde trail. You understand?'

'Yeah.' Cotton nodded automatically. Then realised what the halfbreed was saying. 'No!'

'Yeah,' said Breed.

And his left hand clamped over the severed, slippery surface of Cotton's mouth and pushed the young man back flat on the bed. Cotton's legs came up in an attempt to kick the halfbreed away, but the man was in too close and Cotton could only drum his knees against the hard muscle of Breed's thighs. He tried to use his hands, but the fingers didn't work any more: they were just useless appendages that dangled loose from his hands.

The Bowie knife came down and across.

Over Cotton's belly, just below his navel, there appeared a gaping cut. It was lipped with raw flesh that dribbled redly in the pale light. Curiously, there was no pain. At first. Then there was a fierce burning sensation as the muscle was parted by the second cut, exposing the sac of the interior stomach. A third cut, delicate and precise as a surgeon's work, slit the sac. A foul smell filled the room as Cotton's intestines bulged out from the wound, glistening yellow and blue and pink for a moment before the crimson made everything dark.

Breed stooped over the bed.

'Remember,' he said. 'Tell them I'll be waiting.'

And he was gone.

Cotton began to scream then.

And Maybellene woke up. She heard the screaming and clambered to her knees, clutching at her aching head. When she saw Cotton she began to scream, too.

ELEVEN

'He butchered the kid. Jesus! You saw him, Fargo. He looked like raw meat.'

Fargo nodded and lifted the whisky bottle. Passed it to Jude.

The red-head filled his glass to the brim and swallowed half in a single gulp.

'What we gonna do?'

'Kill him,' said Fargo. 'We're gonna meet him an' kill him.'

'You crazy?' Jude emptied the rest of his drink. Topped himself. 'I say we run. I don't reckon on facin' no crazy halfbreed.'

Fargo's dark eyes bored into the stocky red-head's face. He had downed the better part of a bottle since the ruckus in the whorehouse had brought them running down the street with half of Mattock's population along for the fun, and whisky always made him mean. Meaner.

'Where you gonna run, Jude? Our money's in Valverde, an' them cows are beyond. We want to sell 'em in Grantsville, we hafta go through Valverde. You gonna give all that up?'

'Christ!' Jude shuddered. 'He'll be waitin' for us. Luke's dead. He killed Taggart. Now he's killed Cotton. It's just like you said – he's out for revenge. An' we're on the list.'

'So am I.' Fargo's hooded eyes narrowed down to slits. 'I ain't partial to bein' run outta nowhere. I ain't gonna let no goddam halfbreed spook me.'

Jude thought about it while he drank more whisky. He didn't want to quit Mattock on his own; not with the halfbreed lurking around, maybe ready to pick him off.

Nor did he want to give up his share in the rustled cows. But by God! the 'breed had him frightened.

He tried to find a compromise.

'Maybe we could skirt round him,' he said, conscious of his voice slurring. Whether from whisky or fear, he didn't know; or care. 'Go 'cross the Box M range an' come up on Valverde from the south?'

'He'd come after us,' said Fargo. The whisky didn't seem to affect him, except to make him colder and more dangerous than usual. 'He's proved that already. Sensible man wouldn't have come back to Mattock in the first place, but the halfbreed did. Ain't many would risk lynchin' a sheriff, nor risk comin' in to carve Cotton like that. You don't understand him, Jude. He's Cherry Cow, an' he's made hisself a promise to kill us. He'll do that, unless we stop him.'

Jude stared into his glass, then shrugged.

'So what we do?'

He wasn't very good at thinking, Jude Stoddard. Mostly he was muscle and a fast gun: a useful combination when there was someone to point him in the right direction and tell him what to do. Left to his own devices he tended to mess things up. He was thirty-five years old, six of them spent in the penitentiary after he'd attempted an unsuccessful raid on a bank in Torres Blanco. He'd been with Fargo for close on seven years and got into the habit letting the thin man do his thinking for him. He'd never had so much money as was waiting for them in Valverde – more than he'd expected, now that Luke Masters and Cotton were dead – and he didn't feel like leaving it behind.

Fargo clarified his thoughts.

'We got exactly nine hundred and forty-seven dollars in the Valverde deposit,' he said. 'The cows hafta be worth at least eighty dollars. That makes one thousand an' twenty-seven. Split two ways, we get five hundred an' thirteen apiece.'

'Shit!' said Jude, cheering up. 'I never had that much

money before.'

'An' there's two of us,' added Fargo. 'An' we don't hafta follow the trail. We can go wide. Come in on him from two sides.'

Jude nodded, then frowned: 'How we know he'll be where he told Cotton?'

'He kept his promises so far,' grunted Fargo. 'Didn't he? Besides, that's flat country out there. We got as good a chance of spottin' him as he's got of seein' us.'

'Yeah,' said Jude. 'That's right.'

'Fine,' said Fargo. 'We'll move out tomorrow. We'll kill the bastard an' go celebrate in Valverde.'

The day Cotton Frederick Rockwell got buried was very hot. The sky shone like polished silver plate, the sun burnishing the azure so that no colour showed except the yellow-white orb that fed heat to the land. There were no mourners, just the undertaker and the two Mexican gravediggers; and they didn't stay any longer than it took to drop the rough box into the hole and shovel the dry earth on top. One of them hammered a wooden marker into the ground. It was little more than a plank, with some words scratched over the surface. The words just said: *Cotton. Killed in bed.*

Maybellene had put up the money, from what she found in Cotton's saddlebags. In addition to what he had already paid her, she held back sixty dollars for the fund she was depositing in the bank. She already had almost enough to finance a journey to New Orleans and get a room of her own. That was her ambition, but she put it off for a while because she was suddenly very popular: the local clientele wanted to sleep with the whore who had been there when Breed killed Cotton. Her price went up from ten dollars a night to fifteen.

Fargo and Jude ate a good breakfast. Then they bought supplies for the journey to Valverde and killed a bottle in the Lucky Lady. They rode out of Mattock with

99

Winchester carbines canted over their saddles and their eyes scanning the trail ahead. Fargo had bought a spyglass from Caleb Black, and every so often he reined in and extended the telescope, checking the terrain in front.

Jude had never seen him so nervous.

Breed made camp exactly where he had told Cotton. For the first night. After that, just before dawn, he found another place where an arroyo made a cut across the prairie. He fashioned a makeshift shade for the grey stallion and scattered a pile of oats on the ground. He scooped out a pit in the dry sand and lined it with a section of tarpaulin held down by rocks. He filled the hollow with water and left the horse on a long tether. Then he went back to the original campsite and spread his blanket on the ground. He left his saddle there, and his hat. Around his mane of sun-bleached hair, he wound the leather war-band.

Then he took up station behind a slight rise to the south. He carried his Winchester and a canteen. He settled down to watch the Valverde trail.

From ground level, the rise was no more than a slight hummock that drifted on a north-to-south line across the trail. It dipped where the road went through the centre. Over the flatlands, it gave an excellent view of the western approaches.

'All right.' Fargo reined in. 'We split up here. You move south. Circle round an' then come in from the east. I'll go in from the north.'

'Suppose somethin' happens?' queried Jude. 'What then?'

'It ain't gonna take more'n a day to find him,' snarled Fargo. 'If we ain't killed him by then, we ride for Valverde. Meet up there.'

The *If* hung heavy on Jude's mind, but he didn't say anything. Just nodded and steered his pony off the hard-packed dirt of the trail onto the softer ground to the south.

For a little while, he thought about riding out, straight to Valverde. Then he decided it was best to do what Fargo said. Best to kill the halfbreed and take him off their tails. Besides, he wasn't sure he could get the money out of the bank on his own. It might need a signature for that, and he couldn't write.

And there was another consideration: if he let Fargo down and the hook-nosed man lived, then Fargo would come looking for him. And he wanted that even less than having the halfbreed trailing him.

He rode southwards through a parched landscape of saguarro and cholla and mesquite, circling slowly so that he was sure of passing the place where they had found the halfbreed camped. After that, he moved north and east, coming back onto the Valverde trail before turning the pony's head west again.

He stopped once to eat. And three times to swig from his canteen. Each time he stopped, he drank some more from the whisky bottle he had stuffed into his saddlebags.

He wished Fargo hadn't suggested that trip to Valverde.

Wished he hadn't gone along.

Wished they'd never found the halfbreed.

But now it was too late.

Some hours into the afternoon the whisky bottle shone empty when he canted it to his mouth. He threw it away, wishing he had another. He climbed down from his horse and opened his pants, splashing liquid over the trunk of a cactus. He wasn't, he calculated, more than a quarter mile from the campsite, maybe a bit less. He nodded to himself, whisky-wise, and climbed back on the horse.

By now Fargo should have moved in from the north: the halfbreed would be trapped in a crossfire.

If he was there.

And there was only one way to find that out.

Jude thumbed the hammer of the Winchester back and heeled the pony to a fast canter.

A straight charge, that was the thing. He remembered Fargo telling him how the Texas Rangers handled Comanches: how the Rangers had surprised the Indians by using their own tactics against them. By charging straight in, relying on surprise and fire power.

He forgot that Breed was half-Apache.

Breed calculated the time by the sun. He had never owned a watch, nor ever paid much attention to clocks. The sun was time-keeper enough, and the feel of the land, of the sky.

Round about now, he guessed, the two men should be reaching his position. They were too careful – too canny, his father would have said – to come straight in, so the chances were that they would circle to move in from either side. He thought they would try that because he thought he had frightened them enough to lure them out: to try to take him off their tails.

So he was ready for the sound of Jude's horse as it pounded across the arid prairie. He touched his fingers to the blade of the Bowie knife, feeling a faint vibration stir the metal where it was dug into the ground. He tugged the blade loose and sheathed it on his hip.

One horse, coming fast.

He wondered where the other might be as he folded against the sand, his body hidden under the overhang of a gigantic saguarro.

Jude spotted an arroyo that he guessed would take him up behind the camp site. It was deep enough to hide his approach and when he got to where he thought he was more or less level with the site, he dismounted and began to move in on foot.

He slid his hat back off his hair, leaving it hanging by the leather chin strap. He inched his way up to the rim of the arroyo and saw a flat space in front, lifting up thirty yards distant in a low rise that was dotted along the upper edge with cactus. He checked the flat, then ran across, throwing himself down on the side of the ridge. Then, slowly, working inch-by-inch, he eased up to the rim and peered over.

He saw the saguarro-ringed clearing where they had found the halfbreed. There was a fire smouldering at the centre. A bedroll spread from a saddle, bulky as a man's body might make it. A hat at the top.

He grinned and went back to his horse.

The halfbreed was playing possum. That was obvious. He was waiting with a rifle under his blanket for the attack. But when Jude came charging in, he'd be taken by surprise. Fargo would hear him yelling and come in from the north. Most likely charging the way he'd told Jude. They'd catch the halfbreed between them and kill him. Get it done, so they could ride free to spend their money.

Yeah, Jude shook his head, that was how it would be. Real easy : like Fargo had said. The only thing missing was another swig of whisky; but that would come in Valverde. Plenty of it.

Jude got up on his pony and urged the animal over the wall of the arroyo. He'd never favoured spurs, but he wished he had them now : they might have added an extra turn of speed to the charge.

He slammed his heels against the animal's flanks and went down onto the flat with his mouth open in an ear-splitting yell.

He topped the ridge and went down the far side, Winchester pumping .44-40 calibre slugs into the bedroll.

The blanket danced under the impact. Tufts of cloth flew clear. The low-crowned stetson rolled away.

And Jude swung up the far side of the depression with the awful realisation that it was all a decoy.

Then his horse faltered.

He felt the reins tug loose from his left hand and something warm and wet hit his face. He grunted and began to tug the reins back. They wouldn't come. The pony's head wouldn't move. Instead, it began to drop as the front legs folded.

Jude realised that the wetness on his face was blood from the animal's skull, and shouted : 'Fargo !'

The horse went down. In a weird instant of clarity, Jude saw that a bullet had shattered the animal's head neatly between the eyes and the ears. He kicked out of the stirrups, powering clear of the tumbling body so that he rolled back towards the fire.

The horse snorted, long streamers of bloody foam spuming from its nostrils as the muzzle hit sand and the legs doubled. Its eyes were blank and dead. It shuddered, folding forwards into the ground, then kicked once and began to roll back.

Jude shouted, 'Fargo ! Where the hell are you?'

Then, unthinking, he began to lever the Winchester carbine, spraying bullets in a semi-circle around the clearing.

Sand plumed high into the air. Chunks of cholla and saguarro flew loose from the branches. Smoke filled the depression.

The Winchester clicked empty.

Jude tossed the carbine aside and drew his Colt.

He opened his mouth to yell, 'Fargo !'

But the shout got cut off by the bullet that shattered his left knee. And Fargo didn't answer.

There was no sign of Fargo.

There was only pain and loneliness and heat.

Jude looked at his leg. His foot stuck out at a curious angle, and there was blood staining his pants. More on the sand below him. He rolled onto his right side and began to pump his way towards the nearest big cactus.

He was halfway there when a slug struck his right wrist.

He screamed as the impact burst his fingers open,

spinning the Colt two feet from his body. It had broken his wrist where the arm joined the hand. There was blood pulsing from the underside. Where the artery was severed, and the hand flapped loose, like a limp red flag, there were pieces of bone sticking out.

He rolled over onto his back and tried to reach the fallen pistol as Breed came down into the hollow. There was smoke curling from the barrel of his rifle, and the hammer was full back, his forefinger tight on the trigger.

'Fargo!' shouted Jude. 'For Chrissakes!'

'I think he's gone,' said Breed; slow and quiet. 'I think he left you.'

Jude didn't hear him. All the strength – all the purpose – left in his body was concentrated on reaching the pistol. There was a haze over his eyes. A red haze that washed and flickered through his being like the surging of the ocean he had once seen in Galveston. Something irrefusable, relentless.

He reached for the Colt. It was familiar, an old friend: he knew from the chipped butt and the dented strap.

There was the trigger just beyond the butt. Then the cylinder and the barrel. All he needed do was get his good hand on it.

Fasten his fingers around the butt.

Thumb the hammer back.

Settle his forefinger over the trigger.

Lift the pistol so that it pointed at the halfbreed.

Squeeze the trigger.

He had done it before. Why not now?

Why was his old friend so far away?

He never even felt the pain of the bullet that spread his left hand like a bloody spider over the ground. He just stared at it and laughed, watching the splayed fingers drip crimson onto the sand as they crumpled and folded under while he went on reaching for the gun.

When they got there, they couldn't hold the pistol. Instead, they struck the familiar grip and sent waves of pain flooding up his arm. He screamed.

'Where's Fargo?' Breed asked. 'Tell me.'

Jude laughed; a high, hysterical giggle.

'Valverde's the place. We meet there. Me an' Fargo. No one to share with. Not now.'

'Thanks,' said Breed.

And triggered the Winchester into Jude's face.

The .44-40 slug smashed through the bone structure as the flash scorched away the eyebrows and seared the eyeballs to milky red pulp. It crashed the bridge of the nose inwards so that both eyes got tugged into the hole at the front of the man's skull. Impact bounced the head upwards as the slug imbedded through the rear of the brain into the ground beneath. One eye burst from the socket, dangling on crimson cords over the cheek. The other was lost inside the massive gouting of blood from the rear of the skull.

Pieces of bone and brain matter gusted in a wide circle from under Jude's head, and what was left of his face stared up at a sky he could no longer see.

Flies settled on the body, oblivious of the blond-haired man who stood for a moment, watching them.

When he was gone, they settled in thicker. Until the buzzards came down and began to peck at the corpse.

By morning most of it was gone. What the buzzards left, the coyotes took. After that, there wasn't much left, except for the ants and the beetles.

After a while, Jude Stoddard was just one more pile of bones fertilising the Texas plain with no one to remember him and no marker to state his name.

Fargo watched it happen through his new-bought telescope.

He saw Jude die and grinned as he folded the spyglass back in the case.

It had all gone exactly as he wanted: the only snag was that Jude hadn't killed the halfbreed. That would have made it perfect. He'd thought that maybe Jude had a chance – the red-haired idiot was stupid enough to charge in and take the 'breed by surprise.

So : all right. Jude was dead, but the 'breed was still delayed.

Fargo mounted up and rode hard for Valverde.

With everyone gone, there was upwards of nine hundred dollars waiting, just for him, in the Valverde bank. The cows he'd forget about : it was easier to take money than to try herding steers alone.

He folded the telescope back inside its case and stuffed it down into his saddlebag. There was no one on his trail, just a long column of buzzards circling down towards the body of Jude's horse and the scantier pickings of his deceased partner's corpse.

Fargo laughed and slammed his heels against the flanks of the big black horse he was riding. It would be dark soon, and anyone who didn't know the trail would find trouble.

Good old Jude, he thought, you really did me a favour.

Breed went back to the grey stallion when he was sure there would be no second attack.

He saddled up and checked the ground. And after a while, found where a man had watched the killing of Jude Stoddard. He knew the watcher had to be Fargo, so he followed the spoor the man left.

It headed out through the dry country in the direction of Valverde. When the tracks met the road, they got lost inside the slurring of wheel ruts and cattle herds, but the direction stayed obvious.

Breed rode eastwards, confident of catching up with the thin man in the town.

He rode slow, not wanting to spook Fargo. Wanting to let the man believe he was clear. Wanting to let him feel safe, so that the final confrontation would be that much more terrifying.

He camped out one night, knowing that Fargo would

be running harder, confident of his own abilities as he remembered something old Sees-The-Fox had told him.

A running man is frightened, the old hunter had said. *He has two paths to watch, after all. One is in front of him, the other behind. He must look for a way of escape from the one who follows him, and watch behind at the same time. That is difficult: no one has eyes both sides of their head. For the hunter, it is easier: he can see where his quarry is going, though he has two choices, as well. Easier choices, though the outcome depends on his judgement: to drive the game before him, or to move in front and take it there.*

If he is a good hunter, the choice depends on him.

Breed chose the latter path as he closed on Valverde; to get in first and wait over for his quarry.

Fargo wore out his pony midway between Mattock and Valverde.

The horse faltered, spluttering blood-flecked spume as its head drooped and its forequarters folded up. Fargo slid clear of the saddle, landing on his side as the tilt of the animal threw him clear.

He stood up and began to lash the reins about the pony's head. After a while, the animal climbed to its feet again. Fargo swung into the saddle and felt it go down. The horse snuffled froth, and he was thrown over again.

He shot the horse, more from anger than compassion, and left it on the trail. He took his saddlebags onto his shoulder and carried his Winchester in his left hand as he began to walk down the Valverde road.

The sky was getting dark. Over to the west, the sun was fading down behind the horizon. It shone red out of the western hills, temporarily filling the flatlands with burning red-gold light. Box M cattle lowed a sad, belling lament to the dying brilliance.

And a circuit rider stopped his pony on the trail and

stared at the pilgrim wandering down with his bags on his shoulder and a sad look on his face. He watched the man come out of the shadows before he recognised Fargo.

His name was Travis Mather, and he was nineteen years old. He was surprised to see Fargo walking.

'What happened?' he asked. 'You lose yore horse?'

Fargo nodded and said, 'Give me yours.'

Travis Mather shook his head and said, 'Sorry, mister Fargo, but Jonas gave orders about you.'

'What orders?' Fargo asked; knowing the answer already.

'Said you didn't work for the Box M no more,' said Travis Mather. 'Said you was posted clear of Mattock an' the ranch. Said we wasn't to give you anything.'

'Jesus!' grunted Fargo. 'Not even to a man afoot?'

'Well,' said Travis Mather, 'I guess he didn't think of you losin' yore pony. I guess he wouldn't argue about me givin' you a ride back to Mattock, not seein' as how you are afoot.'

'I'd appreciate it, boy.' Fargo extended his hand so that Travis could haul him up. 'That would be a real favour.'

Travis Mather reached down to take the hand.

Then he saw the last thing in his life, which was the muzzle of Fargo's carbine. It flamed yellow as Fargo dragged the cowhand down from the saddle as the Winchester shattered his face.

The muzzle was pressed up close. It burned Travis Mather's hair as his skull fragmented into tiny pieces under the pressure of the .44-40 calibre slug. Blood and brain matter gouted in a column over the cow pony's hindquarters. Fargo held onto the reins until the bucking stopped and the corpse slid loose. Then he mounted and calmed the pony.

Travis Mather slid clear into the sand of the trail. Ants began to crawl into his opened skull.

Fargo looked at him for a moment before turning the pony.

'Thanks,' he said. 'I wish all the cowhands were as brainless as you.'

TWELVE

Valverde was a cluster of adobe buildings around the central focus of the trail. Smaller than Mattock, it had a curiously impermanent air, as though the hot wind blowing up out of Mexico might dry out the white stucco frontages and spread the buildings in powdery dust over the plain. There were few private houses, the majority of the structures given over to stores and saloons and the whore house. There was a plaza at the centre, a square of paved stone with a few dried out palmettos around the edges and a near-dry fountain in the middle. The flags were rutted deep with wheel marks.

On all four sides of the plaza there were saloons, positioned so that they boxed the compass, the fronts facing one another in mute rivalry. Between the saloons there was a general store, a stage office, a saddlery, a stable, a smithy, and a hardware store. The whore house was set back from the rest, surrounded by a high wall that was topped with red tiles.

Breed rode in slow, eyes moving with deceptive casualness as he surveyed the ground ahead. There were a few horses tethered outside the saloons, but mostly the place seemed quiet, basking lazily under the swollen afternoon sun.

He halted outside a place called The Palace and hitched the grey stallion to the rail. The saloon was quiet and cool, a desultory game of poker going on midway down the long, low room and a few men drinking at the bar. He ordered a beer: there was no sign of Fargo.

'I'm looking for someone,' he murmured as the barkeep passed his change. 'Man called Fargo.'

The barkeep shrugged. 'I serve drinks, friend. Not names.'

'Tall man,' said the halfbreed. 'Thin. Got a big nose and dark hair. Wears his gun butt-forwards.'

The barkeep began to polish glasses : 'Sorry, feller. I don't know him.'

Breed emptied the mug and walked out into the sunlight. It was hot in the plaza, the air loud with the rattle of cicadas. He led the grey horse over to the stable, where an ancient Mexican promised to rub the animal down and water it.

'*Por favor,*' Breed said, 'there is a man I want.'

The stablehand shook his head when he heard the description, shaking one liver-spotted hand in warning.

'He is a bad one, that. A *pistolero*. He comes here sometimes to get drunk. He is ugly when he is drunk. *Muy malo. Muy arisco.* I think he stays in the *burdel.*'

'*Gracias.*' Breed left the stable.

He thought about going to the brothel, but decided that Fargo would most likely want to drink before he relaxed with a woman. Would want to get information. He went over to the nearest saloon.

The barkeep in the Valverde Queen denied any knowledge of Fargo.

In The Silver Dollar the man behind the counter said that he had seen a man answering that description, but he mostly drank in The Imperial.

The Imperial was the biggest of the four saloons. It had batwings in place of the bead curtains covering the entrances to the rival establishments, and there was a huge painting hung above the bar. Like the picture in the Lucky Lady in Mattock, it depicted a large-breasted woman in a state of disarray, though here she had red hair and showed more. There was a brass foot-rail running the length of the bar, and spittoons were spaced along the floor.

Breed ordered a whisky and began to ask his questions.

'Fargo?' said the bartender. 'Sure. Comes in every month or so. Got hisself somethin' goin' up around Mattock, ain't he? With the Box M? Why you wanta know?'

'He owes me,' said Breed.

'Ask soft, then.' The barkeep rinsed a glass, grinning. 'Fargo ain't the kinda man pays up easy. He's mean, that one.'

Breed shrugged. 'He always come here?'

'Yeah.' The barkeep nodded. 'Mostly gets a bit likkered up, then heads for Rosie's place. Beat up on a girl there, once. Said she was over-charging him.'

'What the law do?' asked Breed; innocently.

'Law?' The barkeep chuckled. 'We ain't got no law in Valverde. Got a Citizens' Committee, an' the circuit judge comes by 'bout twice a year, but that's it.'

'No marshal?' Breed queried.

The barkeep shook his head.

Breed bought himself a bottle and ordered a bowl of chili. He carried the bottle over to a table set against the far wall. After a while, a fat Mexican woman brought his food and he began to scoop up the spicy mixture of meat and beans with the tacos.

Outside, the shadows lengthened as the sun climbed slowly across the sky. The saloon emptied out until only Breed remained, sipping whisky and staring at the door. The Mexican woman cleared his plates away, and the barkeep began stacking glasses. An old man with rheumy eyes and arthritic hands began to slide a brush over the floor, casting surreptitious glances at the silent man in the shadowy corner.

Somewhere a clock chimed five times. A dog barked.

The barkeep looked up from his tallies and asked, 'You stayin'? We got rooms out back.'

'I'll decide,' Breed shrugged, 'later.'

The barkeep nodded and went back to his figures: there was something about the blond-maned man that made him nervous. It wasn't the kind of nervousness he felt when men like Fargo were around; rather, it was the stillness the man had, like an aura about him. It was as though he would sit there, left hand touching his glass, the right close to his gun, for as long as it took him to accomplish whatever he was planning. Just wait, almost motionless, until he had achieved his purpose.

The barkeep looked up again when hoofbeats sounded outside. A winded horse blew shrill whistling breaths that were drowned out under the thud of boots on the sidewalk. And the batwings flew open.

Fargo came in.

He was dusty, the sweat trickling down his narrow face forming runnels through the coating of powdery sand. He wore his black hat tilted low over his forehead, small eyes glaring angrily about the room. He wore a black shirt and a pair of black pants that were tucked inside the black leather boots. Small silver spurs stuck out from the heels, the rowels dark with blood.

'Whisky!'

He went straight to the bar.

The barkeep's eyes flickered automatically towards the end of the room, and Fargo followed his gaze.

'Jesus!' he said. 'I thought you'd be long gone.'

There was no fear in his voice, only surprise.

'I waited for you,' said Breed. Slow and cold and deadly.

Fargo nodded and lifted the glass. Tossed it down, and beckoned for another. The barkeep filled it, and pushed the bottle forwards. After that he faded discreetly into the background.

'You killed Jude,' Fargo said: a statement. 'He tell you I'd come here?'

Breed nodded.

'I got money here,' said Fargo. 'I don't plan on losin' it.'

'No,' said Breed. 'You wouldn't. Nor did Jude.'

'Jude was stupid,' Fargo said. 'He's dead.'

'He called your name,' said Breed. 'He thought you'd help him.'

Fargo laughed. 'Like I said – Jude was stupid.'

He poured whisky. Lifted the glass with his left hand, the right cupped on his waist, close to the reversed butt of the Colt.

Breed sat watching him, not moving; still.

There was a kind of understanding between them: a mutual hatred that in many ways brought them closer together than friendship. One of them would die. Must die. They both knew that: it was irreversible as the turning of the seasons.

'You should've gone away,' said Fargo. 'That first time. You should've gone then.'

'I didn't,' Breed answered. 'I couldn't.'

'I said that.' Fargo grinned. A cold, ugly expression. 'I said you'd come back.'

He drank more whisky. Then: 'You're part Cherry Cow, ain't you?'

'My mother was Chiricahua,' said Breed. 'Yes.'

'Thought so.' Fargo nodded as if some point had been scored. 'Cherry Cows don't like givin' up.'

'No,' said Breed.

'All right.' Fargo set his glass down. 'Where you want it?'

Breed shrugged, not answering.

'Outside then,' said Fargo. 'In the square.'

Breed nodded and stood up.

The plaza was quiet. A few people watched the two men step out of the saloon, then ducked back inside doorways as they sensed the approaching impact of sudden violence. The air was warm, empty of movement and suddenly still, save for the constant background scraping of the cicadas.

Fargo glanced at the sky, then stepped off the sidewalk onto the rutted flagstones. His boots echoed loud in the silence.

He paced over to stand beside the fountain, the sun behind him, outlining him as a stark, black figure against the red-gold glow.

Breed squinted into the brightness and adjusted the angle of the wide-brimmed Sonoran stetson as he paced over to far side of the bird-stained marble bowl.

'You religious?' Fargo called. 'If you are, you better start prayin'.'

Breed spat a fragment of meat onto the stones. His spittle made a little circle of moisture in the dust. It dried fast, leaving just the stringy piece of meat. Ants began to hurry forwards, oblivious of the drama taking place in the world above them.

'When you're ready,' he said.

Fargo smiled, thin lips parting beneath his beaked nose.

'You're dead,' he called, trying to spook the impassive figure facing him across the few feet of dusty stone. 'I'm gonna send you to hell.'

As he spoke, he reached for his gun.

His hand slid down his waist to fasten on the butt of the Colt's Peacemaker. His fingers fisted on the grip, forefinger sliding inside the trigger guard as his thumb snapped tight on the hammer. The pistol lifted from the holster, swinging round from the reverse position to angle the barrel on Breed's stomach.

He was fast.

Very fast.

The entire movement was a blur of speed that ended with the detonation of the cartridge.

Breed saw the movement and snatched his own gun clear of the holster.

It came up in a single fluid motion that set his hand about the butt of the Frontier model Colt as his forefinger squeezed down the trigger and his thumb dragged the hammer back. He turned slightly as he drew, presenting a narrower target, feet shifting position with the reflex action of long experience. His thumb lifted from the hammer, letting the pin smash down against the firing cap.

Flame and black smoke gouted from the barrel.

He felt something pluck at his body.

Thumbed the hammer back a second time and felt the Colt buck again in his hand.

Fargo staggered.

The three shots rang in echoes from the surrounding buildings.

Fargo grunted as the first bullet tore into his stomach. It went in just above his belt. He felt no pain, only surprise : he had thought he could beat the halfbreed. Had counted on it. And now there was a lead slug ripping through his intestines.

He began to cock his pistol for a second shot, but there was another detonation that he knew was not his. And something picked him up and carried him backwards so that he felt his feet go away from under him and saw the sky swirl in a mad circle above his head.

Then there was an awful shock that jarred his body and filled it with waves of agony.

He realised that he was on his back. There was something hot and salty in his mouth. Something drumming inside his skull. Pressing noisome against his brain so that the sky turned red.

He grunted, 'Oh, fuck !' and tried to roll over so that he could get up on his knees and kill the halfbreed. But his limbs didn't work the way they should. And the red sky got dark. And a frightening, whirling blackness filled his mind.

And he died.

Breed saw the thin man stagger under the impact of the first shot. Saw him double over as the bullet ripped into his belly. Then straighten up as the second hit his chest and burst his heart. He watched Fargo go down, a thick swell of crimson bursting over his black shirt as a pool of the same colour formed under his body.

The gunman lifted up on his elbows, streamers of blood running from his mouth and nostrils. Then he slumped back with his mouth wide open and his eyes staring blankly at the sky.

The ants left the meat and began to pace, inexorably,

towards the corpse. By the time Breed had crossed the plaza, they were inside Fargo's mouth, scuttling busily into his nostrils and eyes, clambering into his ears; covering him.

Breed ejected the spent shells and thumbed two fresh loads into the Colt's Frontier. Then he holstered the gun and turned towards the stable. He got his horse out and mounted up.

'You are not staying?' asked the old Mexican.

Breed shook his head.

'No. What for? I did what I came to do.'

'I guess,' said the oldster. 'But we have a chapel. You could make confession.'

'I got nothing to confess,' answered the halfbreed. 'Except I feel good. And a priest wouldn't want to hear that.'

'No,' agreed the old man. And watched the tall figure ride away.

Breed went south into Mexico for a spell. He drifted around Chihuahua and Sonora before crossing the border again around Nogales, moving up the line of the southern Gila until he struck the high country of Apacheria. Sometimes he wondered what had happened in Mattock.

Not much.

At least, not in contrast with the violent events of his time there.

Jonas Masters held the ranch together for three more years. Then he decided it wasn't worth building up, not without a son to take it over and keep it going. He sold out to an Eastern company that changed the name to The L&M Cattle Association, and went to live in Houston. A year later, he moved to San Antonio. He was still a rich man, but he was also very bored. After two years in San Antonio, he put his old Colt Dragoon into his mouth and blew the back of his skull away.

It was a big funeral.

Sarah Black never did get married. She went on looking after Caleb, but when the L&M took over the Masters spread, the company opened its own hardware store and drove Caleb Black out of business. He began to drink too much, and died a few years later after downing two bottles of whisky in the space of a single evening.

Sarah sold out to the L&M and moved to St. Louis. She lived in a hotel room until a porter found her dead one morning. She was eighty-seven years old.

Fargo got buried in Valverde's Boot Hill. The three hundred dollars he had on him were taken by the Citizens' Committee to cover the costs of the funeral. There was no proper marker, just a wooden slat that carried the legend: *Plot 31. Fargo*. The money in the deposit got claimed by the stage office – which was the nearest thing Valverde had to a bank – after a year.

The only real memory that remained of any of them was the legend that grew up around the killings. It got spaced out, inflated, so that the town lived a long while after its time on the proceeds.

They called it the Slaughter Time.

BETTER TIMES THAN THESE

BY WINSTON GROOM

The shattering classic novel of a dirty war

'Bravo' company, U.S. Seventh Cavalry. Raw recruits and
ambitious commanders. Men with the tradition of General
Custer and the Indian wars behind them. This is the story of
another bloody chapter in American history: the battle of
Ia Drang valley, and of the soldiers who fought there. But it is
more than the story of those soldiers: it tells of the world –
and the women – they left behind them, and of what happened
when they came up against the horrors of combat. It shocks,
horrifies, moves and enthralls – because it always tells the
raw truth.

'A mirror of hell that leaves one awestruck'
NEW YORK TIMES

'A thoroughly realistic portrait of men at war . . . frightening
. . . genuinely merits comparison with James Jones'
PUBLISHERS WEEKLY

WAR   0 7221 4100 9   £1.75

WAR STORY

BY GORDON McGILL

Berlin, April 1945.

The city – and Germany – is only hours away from final defeat. Deep in the underground passages of the burning city a four-man British unit is fighting a desperate battle against time. Its top-secret mission: to bring a German general back alive, whatever the cost. And to keep one step ahead of the advancing Russian army.

But why?

Find out in WAR STORY

IT'S THE WAR STORY TO END ALL WAR STORIES

WAR FICTION   0 7221 5901 3   £1.00

A SELECTION OF BESTSELLERS FROM SPHERE

FICTION

CALIFORNIA DREAMERS	Norman Bogner	£1.75	☐
HEART OF WAR	John Masters	£1.95	☐
TUNNEL WAR	Joe Poyer	£1.50	☐
LOVING	Danielle Steel	£1.50	☐
REVELATIONS	Phyllis Naylor	£1.50	☐

FILM & TV TIE-INS

THE FUNHOUSE	Owen West	£1.25	☐
THE EMPIRE STRIKES BACK	Donald F. Glut	£1.00	☐
BUCK ROGERS IN THE 25TH CENTURY	Addison E. Steele	95p	☐
LLOYD GEORGE	David Benedictus	£1.25	☐

NON-FICTION

MARY	Patricia Collins	£1.50	☐
EAGLE DAY	Richard Collier	£4.75	☐
THE CLASSIFIED MAN	Susanna M. Hoffman	£1.50	☐
WILL	G. Gordon Liddy	£1.75	☐
MY LIFE AND GAME	Bjorn Borg	£1.25	☐

All Sphere Books are available at your local bookshop or newsagent, or can be ordered direct from the publisher. Just tick the titles you want and fill in the form below.

Name _____

Address _____

_____

Write to Sphere Books, Cash Sales Department, P.O. Box 11, Falmouth, Cornwall TR10 9EN

Please enclose a cheque or postal order to the value of the cover price plus:

UK: 40p for the first book, 18p for the second book and 13p for each additional book ordered to a maximum charge of £1.49.

OVERSEAS: 60p for the first book plus 18p per copy for each additional book.

BFPO & EIRE: 40p for the first book, 18p for the second book plus 13p per copy for the next 7 books, thereafter 7p per book.

Sphere Books reserve the right to show new retail prices on covers which may differ from those previously advertised in the text or elsewhere, and to increase postal rates in accordance with the PO.